Heaven's Fastest Holy Kid

GWENDOLYN SIEGRIST

Looking Forward,

Gwendolyn Siegrist

ISBN: 1530110874
ISBN 13: 9781530110872
Library of Congress Control Number: TXu001983169
Gwendolyn Siegrist, Wichita, Kansas
GwendolynSiegrist.com

This book is dedicated to my family for encouraging me to press on, especially my late mother. I want to thank the many who let me bounce ideas in the story, and all who edited sections for me over the years. I also dedicate this book to parents, families and friends who have lost dear ones too early; I say get your grieve on, but don't stay sad forever. Begin to think of how wonderful heaven is for them right now.

Set your minds on things above, not on earthly things.

—Colossians 3:2

CONTENTS

SPECIAL NOTE TO MY READERS

This story is a work of fiction. Nowhere in the Holy Bible does it describe heaven in the manner and with the detail found in this story. The Bible does not tell us that believers will receive wings and be able to fly. It does not teach us that after arriving in heaven, we will be assigned a mission to accomplish with the empowerment of the Holy Spirit. Believers are not certain that we will know our friends and family in heaven, but we can hope for that—or not. From our earthly perspective, we can hope for the descriptions of heaven found in this story, but I encourage you to read God's Word, accept Christ as your personal Savior, live for Him, and look forward to spending the eternity with our Creator in His heaven. If you want to know how to become a Christian, the steps to salvation may be found on page 78 in this book. I believe the most difficult loss is that of a child, but if God has called your loved one to heaven early, may your grief be lightened by the word pictures found in this story—a story I believe God gave me to help with loss. I wrote this book after losing eleven friends and loved ones in five years, a few of whom were children. I pray that this story will find its way into the homes and lives of families who have lost children or are grieving for such losses.

PROLOGUE

High above the earth on the very edge of eternity, some will find the landing at the entrance to heaven. It is here that St. Peter works, greeting people as they arrive at heaven's gates of pearl.

It is here where I also spend a great deal of time in a tower so high that I can see the earth and all the way to God's throne. My name is Gabriel, and I'm an archangel, a servant and messenger of God.

It is my job to learn from God who is coming to heaven next, deliver his or her set of wings to St. Peter, and then blast my trumpet and announce to all of heaven who is about to arrive.

In between the arrivals, I travel to earth to make special announcements for God or attend meetings, feasts and ceremonies here in heaven, or do special tasks for God. At other times I join St. Peter out on the landing, where we sing praises to God and often share our excitement over the newest arrival.

Of course, every arrival in heaven is a special, blessed event, but since we know everyone before they arrive here, some stories are more interesting. I'd like to share with you one such story.

1

THE ARRIVAL

I had just delivered the wings, blown my trumpet, made the announcement, returned to my tower, and began watching as heaven prepared for the welcoming of young Ryan Allen. The Holy Kids' Choir gathered inside the gates of pearl, while angels gathered outside. Full of excitement and eager to do his job, St. Peter began pacing around the landing.

"Gabriel, you know this is when my heart speeds up with excitement," said St. Peter.

"And your hands are getting sweaty from your tight grip on the wings?" I asked.

"Of course." He stopped at the landing's edge to search for any sign of the new holy kid on his way to heaven and then looked down at the wings. St. Peter ran his hand across the beautiful feathers and said aloud, "Every task in my job is my favorite, thank you, God, but somehow I love doing this one the most. I can hardly wait to put these on Ryan. He'll be so excited." He said to the angels, "We might have to hold him down to keep his feet on the floor!"

We all laughed, and the angels nodded their heads in agreement. Even in heaven, Ryan was a kid known for moving fast.

A second later, St. Peter spotted a flash of light traveling from earth toward heaven at an astounding speed—faster than he'd ever seen before.

Thirteen angels with gigantic wings were escorting it, but St. Peter noticed that even they could not keep pace with this new arrival.

"That's got to be him. It is him!" St. Peter turned and shouted through the gates of pearl to the crowd of holy kids who waited with the same anticipation. "Get ready. Ryan is here!"

Scores of angels gathered beside St. Peter just in time, and the holy kids beyond the gate barely contained their giggles.

The fast runner-turned-holy kid approached the landing and sat down, followed by the band of large-winged and slightly winded angels.

St. Peter was glowing all over as he bent down and firmly took Ryan's chin into one hand. Finally, he could see the light-brown hair, long eyelashes, and freckled nose up close.

Looking squarely into the youthful round face, St. Peter paused for a moment, slowly nodding his head. "You *are* fast, young man. I've never seen anyone outrun his guardians."

Ryan looked around, amazed by his new surroundings. To his left and right stood large-winged angels with sweat beads on their foreheads, and right in front of him stood a peaceful-looking man who was squeezing his chin and mumbling something about him being fast.

"What a fresh dream," Ryan whispered. "If I am dreaming, I'm not going to pinch myself. If this is a dream, I don't want to wake up. I smell an adventure!"

Then he took another slow look around.

"Wait a minute," he said, popping his chin loose from St. Peter's grip. "One minute I'm out jogging, and the next I'm standing in the presence of…of…angels? The last thing I remember before arriving here was a squealing sound like tires on pavement that kept getting closer and closer," Ryan said.

His eyes shot back to the angels. This time he noticed their smiles that reassured him everything was okay.

With wide-open eyes and a grin of his own, Ryan reached up and touched the warm, friendly face of the man in front of him and slowly asked, "Am I…? Is this…? Are you St. Peter? *The* St. Peter?"

"I am," replied the tall, smiling St. Peter. "See this book?" St. Peter held a medium-sized thin golden book in one hand and was tapping it with a finger from the other. He opened it and pointed to a page. "Your name is written right here in the *Lamb's Book of Life*. You are in heaven."

Ryan looked at the opened page and saw his name written in gold ink.

"And right up there"—St. Peter pointed to my tower—"is Gabriel, archangel and messenger of God."

I waved from my tower and called out, "Welcome to heaven, young Ryan! We are excited with your arrival. I will be keeping a watchful eye on you as you adjust to this glorious place. We're so happy you are here!"

Ryan waved to me and then looked again at the thirteen angels. He couldn't help but stare at their bluish-white eyes. Suddenly he gasped, pointing to them, and shouted, "Those guys. Hey, they were...I know them!"

The guardians laughed but said not a word.

"You should recognize them," said St. Peter, and he laughed. "They were your guardian angels on earth. The first one was given to you on the day you were born, and another was sent to you on your birthday each year. That's why there are thirteen of them, Ryan, and you had only twelve birthdays. They played with you as an infant, helped you learn and remember things like schedules and prayers, and were always there to encourage you to do good. They never left your side. And they just escorted you here."

As Ryan looked into their faces, he said, "I remember seeing you all the time when I was little, and thought you were a just part of me." Pointing to the first one Ryan said, "I remember you the most because you were so tall, and had thick, wavy red hair pulled back into a long braid. Your wings were so large that the outer feathers curled under. You used those feathers to tickle my face when I laid in my crib."

"And you," he said to the second guardian, "you had soft skin. I used to touch your face and laugh when my baby fingers would disappear deep into your dimples." Ryan looked into the eyes of the remaining eleven guardians and said, "Oh, I loved you all—each one of you took the best care of me in your special way. But as I grew older and learned more about myself and the world, I must have forgotten you."

His hand resting on Ryan's shoulder, St. Peter interrupted. "You will be able to visit with them later, but now they will be given new assignments and will return to earth to be about the Father's business. Other children will need them."

Ryan said, "I'm excited for those children because these guardians were lots of fun and were very trustworthy angels. You guys were so good to me that I can't express what I'm feeling right now, so I will just say thank you for everything. You guys were amazing, and I love you."

The angels closed their eyes and nodded their heads as if to say, "you're welcome." With their huge wings spread wide, the thirteen guardians lifted up and flew over the gates of pearl into heaven to receive their new orders. A rush of cool wind blew across the landing as they passed.

Ryan turned and looked out into the heavens through which he had just flown so quickly. With both hands holding his head, he said, "I think I need to sit down. I feel dizzy. It must have been my trip up here."

Ryan instantly found himself sitting in a beautiful golden chair that was just his size. His knees bent at the edge of the seat, and his feet flatly touched the…the floor of heaven?

"This must be the kind of floor my mom always wanted. She said it would make her kitchen like heaven!"

But as he looked, Ryan could see that the floor was made of highly polished triangular shapes all fitted tightly together. It was made of gold and had patterns of wings and crowns embossed into them. Clearly Ryan was admiring the triangles when he noticed the brilliant glow standing in front of him. He jumped up and found himself looking into the kindest, gentlest face he had ever seen. Ryan could see the warm smile, the deep piercing blue eyes and cried out, "Jesus? Are you Jesus?"

"Yes, Ryan Allen," Jesus said. "It's me, Jesus."

"Jesus!" Ryan's voice rang with confidence as his little body slammed into Jesus for a deep hug. The two held on tightly as pure love was exchanged. When Ryan stepped back, the two clasped hands and shared a smile.

"Welcome to heaven, Ryan. If you're feeling a little lightheaded it's because you are a new creation. Your body doesn't weigh what it did on earth, and you're not what you used to be." He laughed.

With his eyes the size of saucers, Ryan replied, "When you hugged me, I felt a peace pass right through my whole body! It felt so warm and cozy that I thought I might fall asleep!"

"Well, you're a citizen of heaven now, a 'holy kid,' and trust Me"—Christ leaned close to Ryan—"you will love it all."

Jesus stood tall and raised His right arm toward the choir and said, "And this is the Holy Kids' Choir, here to welcome you home, Ryan."

Heavenly music filled the air, and voices began singing. The sound came from behind the Lord, the angels, and St. Peter, from the other side of the gates of pearl, just inside heaven.

"Well that's cool music," Ryan said, "it's even better than the sound from my iPod!"

Several of the choir holy kids waved at Ryan, and he waved back noticing that they seemed about his size and age.

Jesus and St. Peter could tell that Ryan was anxious to investigate, so the voice of St. Peter quickly refocused Ryan's attention.

"I know you're probably anxious to meet them and go investigate your new home, Ryan," he said before purposely clearing his throat, "but first things first, son. Now, here. These are for you."

Ryan saw the set of white wings in St. Peter's hands, and his eyes seemed to glisten as he reached out to examine them. He could see that every feather was perfectly in line beside the next. He saw millions of tiny, white, flawless feathers all stuck tightly together.

"You must have used hot glue on these," he said.

Smiling, St. Peter readied the wings and placed them around Ryan's shoulders. Miraculously, they were a perfect fit and instantly became a part of his body.

"What, no Velcro?" Ryan inquired.

St. Peter rolled his eyes, and Jesus smiled and responded, "You're in heaven now, Ryan. We don't cut and paste around here. We do things right the first time."

Ryan's face glowed with excitement as he rocked his shoulders to get the feel of having wings attached. He pictured himself slicing through the air like a Learjet.

"Thanks, Jesus." Ryan's eyes sparkled. "It's just what I've always wanted," he said—and he meant it.

As those words fell from his mouth, Ryan fell to his knees. There was no mistaking who stood before him now! It was the "I am that I am": Almighty God!

While helping Ryan up with His mighty hand, God said, "Ryan Allen, welcome to the kingdom of heaven."

Smiling, God wrapped His almighty arms around the little holy kid and held him for a moment.

From my tower I watched this precious moment of union. Ryan seemed to melt into God's arms. We see this every time, with every new arrival. It is always joyful to watch, as Our God is pure love and kindness and His hugs are the ultimate.

God released Ryan from the hug and said, "Your job on earth was well done. You trusted My Son as your Savior and showed My love and peace to many."

"Thank You, God." Ryan smiled and paused. "That was the best hug I've ever had. If all the good times in my life were added to all the love and happiness I felt on earth and then were multiplied by one hundred, it could never compare to that hug from You, God! I can't describe that, so I'll just say it's an incredible God hug that no one can give but You. Thank You, God."

"You are welcome, Ryan. You're welcome for the hug and you're welcome here in heaven. You've earned it all, Ryan, by believing. Now your reward and your mission awaits you here in heaven."

A brilliant white sheet of fabric was draped over God's shoulder. Ryan could see that it seemed to flow like water even as it lay still. Then God took it into His mighty hands and spoke again to Ryan.

"This white robe I give to you because you are My child, and I am your Father. It is part of My robe and was created just for you. Wear it now and forever because of your trust in Me and My Son, Jesus, and in honor of the faith and love you showed to many on earth."

The Father and His Son, Christ Jesus, together placed the white robe gently over Ryan's head. It fell into place around his wings and just above his feet. Again, like the wings, Ryan could see that it was a perfect fit.

From my tower I watched and felt a part of this glorious event. The expression on Ryan's face brought sweet tears to my eyes. He really did live his life for God. He earned those wings, and deserves the gift of his robe. It's an important part of the beginning of his blessing and reward. I thanked God for sending Jesus to earth to save the people from their sin.

God's gentle voice continued, "You lived an obedient life on earth, Ryan, by taking Christ as your Savior. But the time has come for you to join Us. We have a need for someone who is fast, and you were created to help Us with a difficult mission back on earth."

With a big grin, and looking straight in the faces of Jesus and God, Ryan quickly lifted his new white robe to present his old, reliable cross trainers, and proclaimed, "With these Nikes and my can-do attitude, I can conquer any challenge and win any race—despite the small hole in the left sole."

But when he proudly looked down, he was startled to find that his feet were bare. His eyes bulged, and he shouted, "Oh, no! Where are my Nikes?"

A smile spread across God's glorious face, followed by His compassionate and loving laugh. He knew about the hole in the Nikes, and He also knew Ryan's thoughts.

"Ryan Allen, you have no need for shoes anymore. Nike makes good running shoes, but they didn't make you fast on earth. You were fast because you practiced and strengthened the gift of running that I gave to you."

Ryan smiled with relief.

"You obeyed when I told you to run," God continued, "and I blessed your body with unique speed. You will use your wings now, not the Nikes with the hole, and you shall be able to do everything I ask of you."

Making sure he had it right, Ryan asked, "Ok, I'm a fast holy kid without my holey Nikes?"

"You got it," Christ answered, laughing with everyone.

Ryan closed his eyes and laughed too, whispering "I'm so glad there's humor in heaven!"

"We heard that, Ryan," Christ said, still chuckling. "Remember, our Father and I created the sense of humor."

The laughter continued at the landing, and we all watched as St. Peter reached deep into the pocket of his robe.

2

BEYOND THE GATE

Although made of pure gold, the key that St. Peter pulled from his pocket was plain and simple. It was straight and narrow. At the key's end, one notch had been cut away. St. Peter inserted it into the keyhole, and, with a quick flick of his wrist, the gate flew open.

As God Almighty and Jesus Christ walked through the open gate, Jesus turned to Ryan and said, "We will talk again in the Great Hall."

Ryan looked surprised at this statement, but before he could say anything, Christ and the Father turned and walked down a street of gold, stopping briefly to hug holy kids before they were on their way and out of sight.

St. Peter put his arm around Ryan and walked him through the pearl gates and onto holy ground. "When you hear the bell ring three times, go to the Great Hall for the celebration feast where you'll take your first meal. You will meet the Bible saints, you may bring a guest, and Gabriel is coming," he said smiling at Angela. "Afterward you will meet with Jesus, St. Andrew and Gabriel over in Crown Hall and receive the details of your mission. I know you and the others are anxious to try out your new wings now, so have fun, and remember to listen for the bell."

Smiling and nodding his head, St. Peter patted Ryan on the back and said, "Welcome home, Ryan." He then returned to the landing. Ryan watched as the pearly gates closed. Several angels flew over the gate to join St. Peter.

As Ryan turned around and looked at the young choir of thousands, the angelic voices stopped singing and began cheering and whistling. This kind of sound is not found at football games or concerts on earth; it's only found in heaven. Ryan was stepping into a real celebration!

Suddenly these holy kids were everywhere. Some ran directly over to him; some hovered above him. Others flew in circles in the sky, tumbling and spinning in all directions, some calling his name or praising God for all creation.

They shouted greetings like, "Welcome home, Ryan," and "Ryan, we've been waiting for you," or "Ryan, you're going to love it here!"

He was surrounded by thousands of other holy kids just like him, and he stood very still, watching in full amazement. From my high tower, I could see that Ryan was excited, and probably felt full of goodness. I saw tears gathering in his eyes as he wiggled his wings and felt fabric of his new robe.

"Tears in heaven," he asked out loud as one rolled down his cheek?

"But these are different." A young holy girl caught Ryan's tear on her finger and dropped it on her lips. "These are tears of joy, and they taste so sweet. They can only be found in heaven."

A smile spread across Ryan's face, and he asked, "Who are you?"

"My name is Angela," she said, smiling back.

"Oh. Well, look, Angela, I'd love to share tears with you sometime, but what I really need right now is the instruction manual for these wings," he said, pointing over his shoulders with his left thumb. "I'm ready for a test flight."

Ryan watched other holy kids flying everywhere, some quite fast and close to his head. "I'm ready to do that," he said.

"Manuals are for those in training on earth," she explained with her eyebrows going up and then down. "You are in heaven now, remember. You'll learn to think differently after you finish your mission. Anyway, just *think* about flying, and you'll be doing it," she said, again with those eyebrows up.

So Ryan did a little hop to lift himself off of heaven's floor, and he was up. Then he stretched over to the right and his body moved that way. He then moved the other way, then up a little, then down and all at once and found himself whirling around in circles. Her words were true!

"Whoa!" he shouted.

Suddenly he was flying all around the sky, but he was upside down and spinning out of control. There was no slowing down for Ryan. Even as he was learning to fly, he was fast.

More holy kids joined him in the air and laughed hard as they watched him gyrate as they themselves had done at first. The laughter of thousands of holy kids bellowed across the skies of heaven as they dodged Ryan's wild flight patterns. But Angela was always there to reach out and help him regain control and laugh along with him.

Ryan's heavenly body was very different from the body he'd had on earth. Not only could he fly now, but he may find that even a simple jump had so much more power in heaven.

"Angela, I was a really fast runner on earth, so now I want to learn to fly one hundred times faster than that."

"Well I can teach you everything you need to know," she laughed. "Ready to bounce?"

The holy kids took off, Angela was in the lead, and Ryan wobbled right behind. They flew a far distance from the landing to a forest area that had a few snow-covered mountains. Angela asked Ryan to sit on a snowy, rocky ledge while she introduced what she called the basic aerobatic maneuvers. She flew a distance from him and began.

First she did a few barrel rolls, then spiral turns, several loops and a lazy eight. She barnstormed through some trees and came out, ending with a hammerhead stall, and circled back to get her student.

"Well, what do you think?" She asked with her head rocking and eyebrows way up.

Mouth hung open and in total amazement, speaking one word at a time, Ryan asked, "How. Did. You. Learn. To. Do. That?"

"Practice. And learning from the best teachers. Plus," Angela smiled, "Plus, I've been here a while."

A slow grin grew across Ryan's face.

"You ready?" She asked.

"Maybe. I mean, YES!" And with that, he streaked away into the sky, Angela right behind him.

The two holy kids flew through the skies practicing the cool moves Angela knew. I could see that Ryan would be quick in learning to command his new wings, and for the first time, I saw Ryan's speed result in a thin blue streak across the sky.

"You're a natural at flying, Ryan, like you were at running on earth," Angela told him. "You have good balance and you easily keep your head in the right position. Of all the new holy kids *I* have taught to fly, you seem to understand it almost automatically. You're doing great!"

They continued flying until Ryan seemed more comfortable with his new skill, then they decided to take a break.

With wings fully spread, I watched Angela take Ryan's hand to help him gently touch down on the edge of a high cliff that overlooked a deep bay of clear water. They sat down at the cliff's edge and hung their bare feet over the edge. Even from some two hundred feet above the water's surface, fish could be seen. Their colors of gold, blue and orange were brilliant against the white rocks that lined the bottom. Some swam in large schools, while others swam alone.

"Oh, my," Ryan exclaimed. I've never seen a lake more clear and beautiful, not even in Colorado! Do we get to go fishing in heaven? On earth I spent lots of summer afternoons fishing with my brothers at a lake near our home."

"We can dive off of these cliffs and swim here anytime we want, Ryan. Let me tell you about the pure water in heaven. This is the Crystal Sea," she began. "All the water in heaven flows from the foot of God's throne. This particular sea is where God casts forgiven sin when people become born-again believers and give their lives to Jesus. He forgives them and throws their sin in here, where it dissolves. Then He forgets it. Their sins are forgiven forever." Smiling, she looked at him and said, "This water is perfect, and yes, Ryan, the fishing here is really good."

Ryan picked up a small, flat rock beside him, one perfect for skipping across water, and held it tightly with the tips of his index finger and thumb. When he looked back at the water, he noticed that the Crystal Sea was perfectly still except for the rings that came from fish surfacing to sip a breath of heaven's pure air. Ryan pointed that out to Angela and said, "I remember someone telling me that those rings represent rings of love and they don't just stop at the water's edge. No, they encircled the entire globe and could be compared to God's infinite love for us." He laid the rock back down and looked at Angela.

"I have a question, Angela. Did you and all the other holy kids get to heaven the same way I did, by an accident?"

Looking deep into his eyes, she answered, "We all got to heaven the same way, Ryan, but it was not 'by accident.' No one gets to heaven 'by accident.' There's only one way to get to heaven, and that's by accepting Jesus Christ as our personal Savior and believing that He is the Son of the living God. Only those born again through Christ's blood will get into heaven. How we lived our lives and whom we chose to serve makes the difference. The way we are taken from earth is not important, but where we go afterward is!"

"I understand that, Angela. When I was six years old, I realized the difference between right and wrong. And when I was eight years old my parents took me to hear a visiting missionary teach at our church. She said that God loved people so much that He had sent His Son, Jesus, to earth to offer forgiveness for mistakes. That missionary said that if people would believe in Jesus and take Him as their Savior, we would have eternal life and go to be with God in heaven when we died. So, that very night, I, and many other people said yes, and trusted Jesus as our Savior and became born-again Christians simply by believing. We were even baptized, right there on the spot. From that moment on I knew God was with me, right beside me, in me. I always felt protected and never alone."

Ryan looked far out across the forgiving water again, and then he saw it. Smack in the middle of the sea was a cross—the old, rugged cross upon which Jesus had been crucified.

"By way of that cross, I came to heaven." Then Ryan jumped to his feet, stood tall, spread his wings full, cupped his hands around his mouth, and he shouted across the sea and into the sky, "God bless my parents! God bless that missionary! Bless them again and again, Father! For they took the time to make sure I learned Your ways!"

With a smile that also seemed to shout and cheeks dripping with those special tears, he took Angela's hand and pulled her to his side. There by the Crystal Sea, they shared the tears of joy, and their laughter rolled like thunder through the heavens. The sound of a great bell could be heard ringing in the distance.

3

THE FEAST

As Ryan entered the Great Hall, he looked around the room, admiring the pastel-colored scenes of heaven painted on the walls and ceilings. The room was mostly filled with dining tables and chairs. At the head table sat God Almighty and His Son, Jesus Christ, speaking quietly, each nodding His head from time to time in agreement. There were other guests seated throughout the room. Angela, Ryan's guest, explained that they were the biblical saints, great missionaries and two archangels, Michael and me. We waved at the holy kids, and Ryan pointed over his shoulder and mouthed the words to me, "I love these fast wings!" I laughed and nodded my head.

The dining tables were identical in size and were draped with purple cloths of linen that matched the napkins. Each item in the place settings was made of gold, and there were ornate designs around the edge of the plates and on the handles of the forks, spoons and knives. Every table had a centerpiece of three purple candles surrounded by fresh yellow flowers.

The serving tables covered the east side of the room and were loaded with heavenly food. The aroma is enough to make any mouth water, but it must have been the smell and the sight of this delightful feast that made Ryan begin to hover just above the floor, ever so slightly.

"No wonder the saints are looking so pleased," he whispered to Angela.

She reached up for his hand.

"Get a grip, Ryan," she said while waving and returning a smile to St. John. She pulled Ryan back down to the floor and shared her smile with him.

All the saints, angels, guests and Jesus stood with God as He invited Ryan and Angela to be seated at the guest-of-honor table. As the two made their way to their seats, and sat down, God said, "Let there be feasting."

Ryan and Angela were asked to lead the line through the buffet. The table with salads and fresh fruit was first, then meats and vegetables. They piled their plates full, and headed back to their table, where bread, butter, and the most incredible desserts lay inches away from them.

His mouth stuffed full with the first, much-anticipated bite, Ryan observed all the others who were now in line filling their golden plates.

Swallowing hard, he exclaimed, "This place is busier than a Sunday buffet at noon. Can we go back for seconds? This is so good!"

Angela laughed and nodded her head, replying, "Yes, you can go back for seconds and eat as much as you want." Then she scooped at least half a cup of butter onto his plate to make her point.

Ryan asked Angela a lot of questions while they ate, and never once did she say to him, "I don't know." She had an answer for his every wonder.

It was clear to see that Ryan looked very comfortable with his new-found, very wise friend who could fly like a stunt pilot.

They made plans to go flying again and to drop by the Crystal Sea to fish, but first he would need her help to find the Crown Hall, where he was scheduled to meet with Jesus, St. Andrew and me after this feast.

Holy people came and removed the empty plates, and others served milk or the richest kind of coffee. From the nearby dessert tray, Ryan chose his favorite, chocolate pie with meringue that stood nearly two inches high.

After everyone had finished, Jesus stood and chimed a perfect C note with His golden fork and crystal water glass. The noise level went from the sound of a Pizza Hut on Friday night to perfect silence. When Christ had everyone's undivided attention, He began introducing Ryan to each guest, one by one. First was King David, who said to Ryan, "welcome, Ryan."

"Thank you, King David. I know that you helped to write the book of Psalms in the Bible, and as a boy, you killed a giant with your slingshot." King David smiled and nodded his head.

Next, Jesus introduced Joseph, who greeted Ryan with a smile and a nod.

"Joseph, I know that your father gave you a coat of many colors. Then your jealous brothers sold you into slavery. But you were so obedient to God that He made you the overseer of a huge kingdom."

"What is written in the Bible about me is all true, Ryan," Joseph said smiling.

Christ continued all the way down the line, introducing each saint, ending with James, Paul, Luke, Peter, then Michael the archangel, and me, Gabriel, although I had already met Ryan. He must have felt consumed with happiness as he heard "praise God Almighty" and "welcome home" from us. I felt it such an honor to sit here sharing space with God; the Listener to prayers, the Great Physician, the Creator of every single thing that ever was. And I wondered how much more Ryan, heaven's fastest holy kid, felt the honor also?

Suddenly Angela slipped her hand into Ryan's and gently pulled him back down a couple of inches to his seat.

"Was I hovering again?" he asked, but this time he knew the answer. They giggled then hushed as Jesus spoke again.

"As you all know," Christ continued, "Ryan was chosen to come and help us because he's so fast. The Father and I have heard many pleading prayers for the youth on earth. Believers are preaching the Word, but fewer and fewer of the people, especially the young people, are choosing to accept and follow the gospel. Or they're simply not hearing about the one, true God who loves them and can supply their lives with purpose, a plan, love, care, protection and eternal life."

"Most schools have banned prayer during school hours or at school functions, thus eliminating the sharing of God's love where children spend a great part of their lives. These children who haven't received the promise of God's Word have grown up now, and many have become parents themselves. They cannot teach their children about My love because they do not know it."

"Now their children are growing up without the truth and with no one to trust. They have nowhere to turn in their times of need. They don't understand the purpose or value of life. They have no love, hope, peace, direction, or guidance. Without these things from the Heavenly Father, they are frustrated, confused and misdirected in life."

"They have a huge hole of emptiness within themselves, and they long for something, but they know not what. These lost children are becoming violent at an alarming rate and have turned to drugs, guns or other weapons, which give them a false sense of security and authority. They don't realize they are trying to protect themselves from others who feel the same frightened way."

"There were plenty of those lost kids in my hometown," Ryan whispered to Angela. "I saw them desperate to be included, desperate for someone to love them, to need them, and to respect them."

Ryan continued listening.

"But I have seen and heard every one of their cries," Christ continued. "When no one else is around to judge or ridicule them, they cry out in their pain and misery. They cry out not for God, because they do not know Him. They are crying out in confusion."

"They want evil to go away from them forever. They want to love and be loved in peace. They wish for everything they do not have, and they have everything they would never wish for. Little do they know that all they could ever dream of having is already a part of the life God can give them. What they crave is the actual lifestyle in heaven. It could be theirs by simply receiving Me and following My ways."

"If they will turn from their sinful ways and trust God, they will have hope for the rest of their lives on earth. They could then begin to build treasures for their eternal lives in heaven, where peace and love were born."

"But they continue to abuse and kill one another, and their lost souls are not arriving here with us in heaven when they die. This is where Ryan fits into the plan. Because he is heaven's fastest holy kid, he can cover a great deal of territory in a short amount of time."

Looking at Ryan, Jesus said, "You will return to encourage the youth in Keyota, Kansas, your hometown."

The applause in the room was loud, and the praises to God began filling the air in the Great Hall. Hands were lifted high to glorify God and His Son.

God stood at the side of Christ Jesus and put His loving arm around His Son as Jesus again chimed the C note on His glass. The room became silent. "Ryan, is there anything you would like to say at this time?"

"Yes, Jesus, I would. Thank you for making me able to run fast, and for bringing me here for this mission. I am pumped, Lord, and as ready as I can be! My pulse is fast and I feel a tingle shooting all the way through my wings! The only time I felt something like this on earth was when my father and I were about to compete in a race. My dad called it adrenaline."

"That sensation you feel in your pulse and wings are what We call a 'quickening of the spirit', Ryan, a gift for such a time as this."

"Thank you Jesus," Ryan responded. "I know that I am able to take on this mission for the lost, for You my Almighty, and for heaven. I promise to encourage the hurting, lost youth in Keyota so that God's truth will be told and they could arrive in heaven when they died, no matter how they die."

"The details of your mission will soon be revealed, Ryan. We will meet again in Crown Hall."

The feast was dismissed, but some gathered around God thanking Him again for sending Jesus to earth to die for human sins and opening the gates of heaven. Others thanked Him for the blessing of their forever home in His perfect heaven.

"This is the most amazing thing I've ever seen. God loves us all. I will never forget this moment, Angela. I can only hope that all those on earth will experience it."

Angela had tears of joy in her eyes as the praising went on. She smiled, took Ryan's hand, and told him that the saints had wonderful stories to tell about their lives on earth, but that their most thrilling stories were from some of their missions when they returned to earth to minister to the lost.

"Do they still make journeys to earth?" Ryan inquired.

"Oh, yes," she said with enthusiasm. "We can all go there anytime we want and anytime we see the need. That's why we all spend so much of our time at the balcony. But when earthly places or situations are so hardened with sin and hate, God calls us when he needs us, as he just did you, Ryan. We each were created for a special, unique reason, and when we choose to trust Jesus on earth, we are His treasure and eternal life in heaven is our reward. Then He empowers us with His Holy Spirit, and sends us from the balcony to do the job. You will understand this better in your meeting."

Just as Ryan took a breath to ask about the balcony, Christ spoke again, thanking everyone for coming. His question about the balcony would have to wait.

The saints and missionaries waved good-bye to Ryan and Angela as they left the Great Hall. The archangel Michael and I were walking out when Ryan said he looked forward to spending time with us later to hear our stories. We both nodded our heads then Michael flew away.

Christ walked over to the holy kids and me, and told Ryan when to arrive at the Crown Hall for his mission details.

Ryan thanked Him for the great feast and for His endless love and concern for life on earth.

Smiling, Jesus bent down to Ryan, hugged him, and said, "I am glad you chose to believe the truth written in the holy Bible, Ryan. Your faith has set you free in heaven."

I stepped over to Ryan and held up my right palm. Ryan immediately gave it a high-five smack, and I told him I would be watching him from my tower. I spread my wings and flew away.

As they parted ways outside the Great Hall, holy kids and tiny, iridescent-winged babies ran and flew to Jesus for hugs. He sat down on the steps with them and began listening to their stories and the exciting news that came with shouts and giggles.

"Who are those little, shiny-winged babies?" Ryan asked, mesmerized by their precious beauty.

"Oh," Angela answered. "They are so sweet! They are the precious little ones who were growing inside their mothers on earth, about to be born. For different reasons, their lives ended before their births. Completely bypassing St. Peter and the gate, they instantly appear before God to receive their special wings from Him." She looked at Ryan. "Because they were never born into the sinful world, they never sinned, and they never needed forgiveness. They are a pure form of life, Ryan. We all love to be with them." Her eyes sparkled as she watched them with Jesus and the others.

"When they're not playing in the waterfalls or listening to stories, they're usually with Jesus's mother, Mary. That is until most of their parents on earth arrive up here to be with them. There are lots of tears of joy in those reunions. You may even see a few of them on earth during your mission. Even though they never lived there, they have a godly impact on anyone they help."

"I could never have imagined that, Angela," said Ryan. "Everywhere I go and everything I see is very different from things on earth. But I am beginning to see the proof that God's love includes everybody and that His plan works for even the tiniest creation. If the parents of these tiny ones knew how loved, how well taken care of, and how happy they were, maybe they wouldn't be so sad for so long. I want to be at the gate when their parents arrive and help them celebrate. I love a good party!"

4

A GOOD LONG LOOK

Angela and Ryan walked down the seven steps of the Great Hall to the street named Gilead, where they turned left and continued on wide, golden walkways. They passed other holy people, walking in couples or groups, who always stopped to speak to Angela and were excited to meet and welcome Ryan into heaven.

"I can't stop smiling, Angela, and this feeling reminds me of how my face felt during sleepovers with my buddies on earth. We would start telling jokes, or silly stories and we would laugh so hard and for so long that our faces would ache," Ryan said. "But here I can't stop smiling and it just feels good!"

At the corner of Gilead and Matthew, I saw the two holy kids turn right and enter a park, and I listened to them. They walked halfway across a stone footbridge and stopped to look around. Beneath them flowed a clear stream of water that connected to a nearby pond.

"There is more water in heaven than I ever thought there would be," Ryan said.

"Heaven has lots of water, Ryan," Angela began, "and this one, like the Crystal Sea, is perfect for swimming, cooking, fishing, or drinking."

Ryan and Angela looked all around the park and could see holy kids picnicking with other holy people by the pure-white shore. Some were building huge sand castles or digging tunnels that weren't caving in. Others were swimming, wings and all!

They could see holy kids feeding geese by hand and others holding kittens and baby ducks in their laps and petting them. Beyond the pond was a great pasture with horses, tigers, and other large animals running together. And nearby, lying side-by-side, were mother lions and lambs playing with their young. Long-eared and short-eared bunny rabbits of every color hopped about on grass the most beautiful shade of green. There were blooming flowers everywhere that had not a trace of wilting or decay. The trees were giant-size, some growing in groves, and beneath them in the shade sat a few holy people reading books. Others walked two-by-two in the light, reciting poems about the majesty of God and His kingdom. Lastly, he spotted a holy dad walking beside a stream with a little boy riding piggyback. Ryan smiled and watched them for a moment, remembering the many times his brother had mounted up on his back, and then away they'd go for a wild ride in the backyard.

Angela pointed out across the park to a sports complex that included a running path, a track, and a golf course off to the right, and cut into a hillside were tennis courts, soccer fields, baseball diamonds, and even a football field, which was packed with players and loudly cheering spectators.

"Do they serve hot dogs and nachos," Ryan asked?

"Yep, sure do," said Angela smiling.

"And look at those holy kids racing down the hillside on their bikes," she added. "They're riding so fast that their wings are pinned back! And flying above them, are other holy kids racing along laughing so hard that they can barely keep up."

"On those mountains back there you can see the snow skiers coming down the mountainside," she looked at him, "but there's no ski lift. You can guess how they get back up the mountain."

"Oh, they're using their wings to fly back to the top!"

"And over here," Angela stepped to the other side of the bridge, "are many mansions that God made for His people."

"Notice how some homes are grouped closely together, but others are farther apart. When I asked Jesus why those homes were not right beside each other, He said they were for holy people who wanted to live out in the country and have horses or a ranch or a farm. Back there are homes close together with porches or patios." Angela turned and pointed to her right. "And the homes way over there that have flat rooftops with cacti growing in the yards, are for holy people who loved earth's desert lands. And all of these, Ryan, are just a few of heaven's mansions God has for His people."

"And where do you live, Angela?" asked Ryan.

"On earth I lived in a very small flat, which was like an apartment that had no yard and no trees. So here I live with family in one of those houses out in the country that have horses and we have fruit trees and a creek that runs in our backyard. How about you, Ryan, where do you want to live?"

"Well, I like lots of trees, too, especially oak trees. I like a big yard where I could have a tire swing and a tree house. And I want to live near Jesus."

"When you get back from your mission, He will put you in exactly the right spot, Ryan, until your parents arrive. He's good at that, especially because you came here by yourself. But I want you to remember that anywhere in heaven is the best place of all. Here we live in complete perfection and can go anywhere at any time. Love, kindness and goodness are what heaven is made of. We are safe, cared for, blessed and kept forever."

"I can see a lot of incredible places from here on this bridge, including homes, horses, holy kids on bikes, and skis. But what I do not see are eyeglasses, hearing aids, plaster casts on arms or legs, no bumps, bruises, scars, or stitches, and I don't see a watch or a Band-Aid."

"Yes, praise God, Ryan. These holy kids play together, all of them healthy, God's children," she said turning to look at Ryan. "And you are one of them, now. Because you believed, you are one of us."

"Come on, Ryan," Angela said. Then the two crossed the bridge and began walking through a patch of tall trees. Looking up, they could see holy kids climbing high and diving out. Just before they reached the ground, they would take flight and squeal from the thrill.

Ryan began laughing, and then told Angela that he wanted to give it a try.

"It reminds me of the Judge Roy Scream, a roller coaster at Six Flags over Texas," he said.

Angela pointed to a holy kid who was about to jump and said, "That's Alex. I sang in the welcoming choir when he arrived here in heaven. When he got his wings, he cried more tears of joy than I'd seen in a long time. It was such a celebration for us all."

"On earth he often parachuted with his father, but one day his chute did not open, and he was badly injured. He spent part of his life in a wheelchair and in a lot of pain. He was very anxious to come up here to be with Jesus. He prayed a lot, and many of us could hear him from the balcony and went to encourage him."

"Finally his time came to join us. Since he's finished his mission back on earth, he spends lots of time jumping and flying and praising God for making him whole again. Ask him sometime what he thinks of his new eternal home, and he will tell you that being with Jesus is the ultimate healing."

Angela saw that Alex was out of the tree and walking with a couple of holy kids, she called out to him.

"Alex! Hey, you guys come and meet Ryan, the newest holy kid."

So Alex and the others came running over, and Angela introduced Ryan to Alex, Jackson, and Lucas.

"We saw you when you got your wings and robe because we were singing in the holy kid choir," said Alex. "We were part of that group of kids who were dodging you when you were figuring out how to begin flying."

"Ha! Well it's nice to meet you guys, and your choir sounded really nice. I saw you dive from the tree just now, and I'd like to hang out with you after my mission. And I think it might be fun to dive from the white rocks at the Crystal Lake. Have you done that?"

Jackson answered, "Yep, we've done that a couple of times, and the cool thing about diving there is that sometimes there's an updraft from the lake. No matter how hard we try to dive into the water, the wind blows us straight back up, so we just float there for a while!"

The gang of holy kids all laughed.

Lucas added, "But then we take off on a race out to the snowy mountains and fly around and see how close we can get without knocking off the snow caps. When you can, you've got to go with us Ryan. We have so much fun."

"We're on our way to Crown Hall for Ryan's meeting," said Angela. "So we'll talk to you guys and make plans later. Bye, and have fun!"

Everyone said good-bye.

As they walked away, Ryan said, "Sounds like they have great adventures. On earth that kind of sporting would probably be dangerous and lead to accidents. Thank God we're here and not still there."

Angela looked at Ryan with her smile and raised eyebrows and said, "Here, we have no accidents. No mistakes can be made, nothing is bad, and no one can do wrong. We holies are free and live to praise God Almighty. Simply put, Ryan, this is heaven, and there is no evil. There is no reason Christians on earth should fear dying."

Ryan remembered Angela's story about Alex and realized that the real story was about God's love and mercy. After watching the holies jumping and swimming and the animals lying in peace, he was again thankful to be part of it all, here in heaven, where there was truly no fear. With sweet tears welling in his eyes, he looked at Angela and said, "I just had no idea how great it would really be in heaven. I guess I never spent much time thinking about it. This place is so incredible."

"You want to see incredible, Ryan? I'll show you incredible. Come on. We're going to the balcony."

She grabbed his hand, and they lifted up, flying east across the real estate of Heaven.

They flew over a group of buildings that looked much like a twenty-first century shopping center on earth made of white limestone. There was lots of limestone back in Kansas where Ryan had lived. In front of the shops ran a small babbling brook and a lot of tall fruit trees shading benches where families and friends sat talking.

Holy kids were gathered around eating what looked like ice cream, only it seemed not to melt or drip everywhere.

"Even though we just ate, that makes my mouth water. I knew there would be ice cream in heaven," he shouted. Angela laughed.

They saw people coming out of another store with books and Angela said it was a library.

"Hey, Angela," Ryan said with a breeze in his face, "think I could get a book about flying, and maybe read it, and I could practice back in the park where the kids were diving out of the trees?"

"Sure," she said laughing. "As soon as you return, we can do lots of stuff. There are many incredible places you haven't seen yet, and, really, there are places I haven't seen yet. Alex can teach you how to dive."

"I can hardly wait," Ryan replied. "Have you been here a long time?"

"Time is not really something kept up with here in heaven, but by earth-time, I've been here about two hundred years," she replied.

"Two hundred years! No wonder you fly so well," Ryan exclaimed.

"You are flying pretty well yourself, and practice is what makes perfect. Your new body is so fast and powerful that it won't take long to understand and control it, but your strength could surprise you." Angela laughed again. "But for now," she finished, "let's buzz by the balcony and then get on to Crown Hall. We don't want to keep our Savior waiting!"

5

THE BALCONY

In the short distance ahead of them was a huge, oval-shaped opening in the floor of heaven. Ryan and Angela sat down on a small nearby hill, which gave them a perfect overall view of the blessed area. Ryan could see that a thick, white, wooden railing encircled the oval opening. There were so many holies bustling about that he could catch only a glimpse of the handrail with its spindles of carved ivy. At the far end of the oval, there was a wide opening where a set of gold-trimmed stairs curved downward and out of sight.

"It's a real balcony," Ryan exclaimed!

"Yes. Awesome, isn't it?" Angela answered as they continued watching.

A large number of excited holy people were present at the balcony.

"The hustle and bustle here reminds me of the busy, thick crowds at the Kansas state fair or my school's spring carnival," Ryan observed.

Some holies stood together in groups, some stood alone, but most were speaking downward through the opening. A sweet, fragrant, misty breeze swept across the area and blew down through the opening, stirring robes and carrying the voices of those who spoke. Ryan saw angels and holies by the dozen fly above them and then dive down through the opening. Then he saw a group walk down those gold-trimmed stairs. Holies standing at the balcony cheered them on with shouts and praises to God.

"It's so exciting to spend time here, Ryan."

"Do you come here a lot?" he asked.

"Oh, yes." Angela nodded her head. "If you're ever looking for me, check here first. Some of us spend so much time here that Jesus calls us 'balcony dwellers.'" She laughed.

"Most of us had the gifts of mercy, faith, encouragement, and leadership when we lived on earth. When we became believers, God allowed us to use our gifts to encourage others to know Christ, too. Well, Ryan, in heaven, it's no different. We can't help but hang out here all the time and encourage *the lost* on earth. It's much more exciting for us now because, as holies, we are part of the body of Christ; we've been touched by God's hand, empowered by His Holy Spirit, and our words have a much stronger impact on humans. We can go anytime and anywhere to encourage them, or work from here. Sometimes this balcony is so packed with holies that there's hardly room to squeeze in, so a whole bunch of us just jump over and make room for others."

"Where do you go?" Ryan inquired.

"Anywhere. Everywhere. Sometimes we go to a Christian concert or a revival. Sometimes we go to help other holies or angels work at bad accidents. I like to work at youth retreats, camps, or sporting events." Touching his arm, she continued, "And it's really neat to go to a home and encourage a Christian who is feeling lonely. I encourage them to read the scriptures, Ryan. I tell them to get down on their knees and really talk to God. I tell them to find a church, and get involved. When they do, they receive great peace. He is always there for them, listening to the desires of their hearts."

"And sometimes, Ryan, I go with several thousand other holies and pack into a church just to hear the scriptures being read. We are filled with God's Holy Spirit, so when we go and minister to others, their faith becomes stronger. Then, as *those* Christians become stronger, they share their faith with others on earth." She slowly nodded her head. "It all works together to glorify our Father. There is always so much work to do, Ryan."

"Are we more powerful encouraging from here or when we go to earth?"

"Oh, good question," Angela, said. "We are very powerful in either place, but sometimes people just need to be held and comforted. And because we are filled with the Holy Spirit, *comforting* is part of our job."

"When you talk to them, do they actually hear your voice?" Ryan asked.

"No. Our words are just thoughts to them. People sometimes say they can hear a still, small voice speaking to them. Well, that is either God speaking to them, or it is we holies encouraging them to seek God. But they have to be *listening* to hear it. Some Christians say it is the voice of the Holy Spirit, and they're right. What we say to them will always be a good or kind thing and will be in agreement with the scriptures."

Ryan considered this for a moment. "Then why do Christians sometimes do bad things?"

"Because they are not praying or reading the Bible. They are still human, and many times they are so busy pleasing themselves that they don't want to stop and listen to the Holy Spirit. They have free will to choose to listen or not to listen for God's voice," Angela explained. "If they *are* listening to a voice and it's not God's scripture-aligning voice, they are hearing evil. They end up making bad choices that don't glorify God or don't set good examples for anyone. Sometimes they are so busy they cannot hear themselves think, so how can they possibly hear a still, small voice?"

Ryan continued watching these holy people who were shouting encouragements down through the opening. Suddenly, a huge group of holies near the far end of the balcony burst into cheers and shouts of praise. They began dancing and swinging one another arm in arm. The air above them sparkled, and streamers shot through the air. Ryan stood further amazed and said to Angela, "That can't be silly string and confetti?"

Overjoyed, Angela looked at Ryan and said, "It is! Another sinner has just been born again."

"Praise God! There really is rejoicing in the presence of the angels of God," Ryan exclaimed!

"You've seen it with your own two eyes," Angela answered.

"Awesome, totally awesome."

"Come on." Angela grabbed his hand and stood.

They climbed down to the balcony and placed their hands on the railing. Ryan listened to a few of the holies speaking down through the opening.

A holy mom and dad were talking to a young woman who could have been their daughter on earth. They were helping her to remember to drop by the hospital on her way home to visit a very sick and unsaved friend.

"Take your Bible, honey," they said to her, "and tell her about God's love for her. Show her the scriptures in the New Testament about being born again. The scriptures are more powerful than your witness. Through faith in Christ, she can have eternal life in heaven when her life ends."

A holy mom stood alone at the edge of the balcony. In her gentle voice, she spoke words of inspiration to a young man, maybe her adult son. She was encouraging him to continue in his faithfulness to God and his family. Ryan heard her say, "Keep seeking God's wisdom, son, and He will show you the way. Your quiet obedience is a powerful example to your family and to the world. Stay focused on what ultimately pleases God."

A holy man spoke to a teenager, encouraging him not to shoplift a CD in the music store.

Then Ryan heard a holy grandmother who was standing at the balcony's edge, reassuring an elderly woman in a nursing home. She said, "Jesus hears your pleas. Keep on trusting Him and keep sharing God's truth with others around you. And stop worrying about me; I am with God in His perfect Heaven."

A holy man stood alone and spoke to a young man who stood in a Christian bookstore trying to decide which version of the Bible to buy. Ryan heard him say, "It doesn't make any difference which Bible you get. Just make sure you read it every day." Ryan saw the friend on earth close his eyes and pick one of four Bibles on a table. He paid the clerk and left the bookstore. The friend at the balcony smiled and said, "Thank you, Lord God."

"Angela!" shouted a holy girl holding on to the rail.

"Oh, hi, Addison," Angela said, waving.

"Look, Angela. My little sisters on earth just got a new baby brother. Look at him. Isn't he cute?" The two holy kids saw Addison's family gathered around, admiring the newborn boy.

Ryan said, "Because I loved babies on earth I want to see your new brother! Oh, he's really cute and he looks so happy. He's got curly hair. And look! I can see he has a huge guardian angel beside his crib. Yeah, that guardian angel is really big, he's, he's, oh my goodness, Angela! Look! That's one of my guardians down there!"

Ryan immediately began filling Addison in on what a great guy that guardian had been to him, and he left out no detail. But Addison was so enthralled with the baby that she could hardly stand still and listen to Ryan. By the time he had finished talking about the guardian, Addison had climbed up and was sitting on top of the railing, both legs dangling over, she was ready to jump. Addison quickly thanked Ryan for sharing and then said good-bye as she flashed straight down to earth.

"Angela, of all the awesome sights I've seen so far in heaven, this one moves me the most," Ryan said. "From here I could encourage my family and my buddies, as I'm sure they're sad about my death. Every day I want them to think about how wonderful it is for me in heaven, and to make sure that they all become a Christian so they will come here when they die."

And Ryan added, "I could tell all the runners to do their best for Jesus and that He would bless them with speed, too. And I could tell the parents of sick and dying children that God knows best and that heaven is a place more wonderful than they could ever imagine."

"The balcony is truly a glorious place, led by, motivated by, and designed by the Holy Spirit of God Almighty," Angela responded. "And you, like all of God's children, will love spending time here."

Ryan was so excited about the balcony that you-know-what happened to him, and you-know-who pulled him gently down to ground.

The two holy kids traveled on, discussing their thankfulness that God sent Christ to earth and that by simply trusting Him, a person could go to heaven when his or her life ended. The holy kids agreed that no Christian should fear dying.

"Especially," Angela added with her arms spread wide, "when the reward for believing is this!"

6

CROWN HALL

Their destination wasn't far off, but the holy kids decided to fly the rest of the way. I saw them landing as I flew to the Crown Hall and sat down in the flower garden to gather a bouquet for our meeting.

Ryan and Angela had touched down beside a cool, inviting water well. Angela dipped her hand in and got herself a refreshing drink, and offered one to Ryan, but he told her that the fortress standing before him commanded his full attention.

"This is Crown Hall? It looks like the Parthenon in Athens, Greece! I saw pictures of it in my sixth-grade geography book, and I studied more about it online when I had to write a paper on it. But the Parthenon didn't have brilliant flowers growing in the garden in front of it," Ryan pointed, "like this one does!"

Ryan spotted me picking flowers, and we smiled.

A porch with huge columns surrounded this massive structure, rectangular in shape. High above the front pillars, in the triangle section of the building, the words "Crown Hall" had been etched into the marble. Real angels sat there on a ledge, talking with one another. Ryan laughed at this because on earth there were buildings with angels on ledges, too, but they were made of stone or concrete.

Across the front porch of the building were planters where more flowers grew. Green ivy, made healthy by heaven's pure light, grew up the front wall of Crown Hall.

Each floor of the building had openings like windows, but there was no glass; heaven's pure air could blow in.

Crown Hall had two massive white wooden doors that could be pushed open and would swing back, closing by themselves. Ryan noticed that there were no handles or locks.

Nodding his head in full approval, he smiled and looked at Angela.

"This is truly the best. No glass, no locks, no darkness, and pure air. My little brother is going to love heaven, and I will tell you why."

"Okay." Angela leaned against the well, crossed her arms, and patiently listened.

"First of all," he began explaining with one finger held up, "he got in a lot of trouble when he broke two windows in Dad's workshop by hitting homeruns in the backyard. And here," he said, pointing to the windowish openings in Crown Hall, "there is no glass to break."

"Next"—finger two went up—"he has four nightlights in his bedroom because he's so scared of the dark. Here," he said, arms open to the sky, "there is no darkness—only heaven's pure light."

"Then"—a third finger was up—"three times last year he lost his house key and had to wait in our tree house until our older brother or I got home with our key to let him in." Pointing toward the closed door of Crown Hall, he concluded, "No locks on doors here."

"And finally, Angela," now folding *his* arms across his chest, "my brother thinks everything stinks, so I know he will appreciate heaven's clean air." To demonstrate, Ryan inhaled so hard that his nostrils stuck together.

Angela couldn't hold back her laughter. She laughed so hard that Ryan was forced to exhale and join her.

Just then a startling burst of laughter came from inside the foyer of Crown Hall.

Angela took Ryan's hand and pulled him to her side. Through a window opening they could see into the brightly lit foyer, where a large crowd of holy people talked and laughed.

"Who are all those people?" Ryan asked.

Angela answered, "It could be any of heaven's holy people and probably a few saints and angels. The saints are often here or at the balcony, and they're always available to talk unless they're gone on a mission. Crown Hall is a gathering place for anyone in all of heaven. It's always open and everyone is welcome."

Ryan took another deep breath of the perfect air and held it for a moment before letting it out. He gently dropped Angela's hand and walked halfway up the front steps.

He turned around and looked at Angela. "I feel like it's my turn in a school spelling bee. If my mom were here right now she would tell me to go wash my face—not that it needs it, but moms are just that way."

"Well won't she be relieved when she gets here, to see that your face is permanently clean?" Then the two holy kids laughed.

Knowing the two would part, he gave her one last smile and thanked her for being such a great friend and helper.

She said to him, "See those mountains over there?" She turned halfway and pointed south. "The River Jordan flows along the base of the highest mountain. There's a nonstop praise-and-worship gathering there. It's really great. I am going there right now to meet with other holy people, including some who were my family on earth." She turned back toward him.

Excitedly, Ryan asked, "So will your mom and dad be there?"

"No. They will not be there. But everyone who is there will be singing and worshipping God, and when I leave there I will be cheering you on from the balcony! If you decide you want company on your mission, just call me. And something very important, Ryan, when you are on your mission, we who stand at the balcony watching you can also hear your thoughts. We can join you in a flash if you want company or need any help."

"I thank God for you, Angela," he said, waving good-bye. He knew again that love on earth could never compare to that in heaven.

I watched as Ryan saw Angela lift her petite wings and take off in a southerly direction to worship the Creator, and I thought those two would be great friends.

7

THE MEETING

For the first time, Ryan was on his own here in heaven, and he was about to have an important meeting.

Although he had been introduced to the Bible saints at the feast, he hadn't had a real visit with any of them yet. He was about to, though, with St. Andrew, Jesus and me.

Ryan smoothed the front of his robe with his hands, prepping, no doubt, to make a good impression. Clearly, he was more than ready.

Ryan looked at the remaining dozen or so steps between him and the porch of Crown Hall and it seemed like he was scheming a little plan. I could see that he was up to something fun, and watched as he turned around and looked over his shoulder and aligned himself exactly in front of the right door. He squatted and pumped his knees—one, two, three, four—and then on five, with all his strength, he sprang up and backward.

Airborne, Ryan's whole body vibrated, and his robe blew straight out in front just like his hair. He looked amazed and quite thrilled at how powerful his jump was. If his plan was to spring backwards up a few steps, he's getting a surprise, I thought! Ryan's body shot past all twelve steps and slammed into one of the closed doors, which flew wide open and smacked against the inside wall with Ryan attached. He slid down the door, making a sound like sweaty legs sliding across a plastic chair in summer, and thumped when he hit the floor.

There he was, sprawled in the foyer of Crown Hall among saints, angels and holies, his robe twisted around his left thigh and hung on the edge of his right wing.

The brilliant conversation inside turned silent as every eye was fixed on the crumpled holy kid who just flew into the room.

I ran up the steps and stood there amazed, looking at the adventurous Ryan.

I heard the sound of bare feet running on marble upstairs, and it was Jesus and St. Andrew rushing out to the banister. They looked below.

The crowd looked at Jesus.

Jesus looked at Ryan.

Ryan looked at his knees, then at me and said, "Hi, there, Gabriel."

"Hello Ryan," I said as I smiled and nodded my head.

And with a smile and shrugged shoulders, Jesus said to everyone, "He's new."

Giggles from the crowd grew to hearty laughter as each one remembered discovering the surprises of their own new heavenly bodies. They could relate. And oh, the stories I could tell!

Stunned by his body's new power, Angela's words must have been ringing in Ryan's ears: *Sometimes your strength will surprise you.* He began to laugh as Jesus came and with His strong hand pulled Ryan to his feet.

Ryan looked into the compassionate eyes of Jesus and said, "I can't explain it, Lord. I just wanted to take a little jump backwards, a couple of steps at a time..."

"No need for explanation," Jesus said, laughing. "Everyone in all of heaven did this sort of thing as they learned to control the awesome power of their new bodies. We all do a lot of learning and laughing together, but I must say, Ryan, watching you learn with your gift of speed will be great fun for us all."

Jesus and I exchanged looks and grins and just raised our eyebrows in humor.

The three of us began climbing the winding stairs that led to the first conference room on the balcony. As we approached, Ryan saw St. Andrew still leaning over the railing, talking with St. Matthew below. We could overhear them making plans to go fishing the next day.

As Ryan climbed the last step, St. Andrew greeted me with a handshake and Ryan with wide-open arms and a snugly hug.

"The only one who had ever hugged me like that was my dad back on earth. St. Andrew, are you a daddy?"

"Uh-oh. The secret's out," St. Andrew said with a laugh. "Did my hug give it away? Yes, I was married on earth and had children, Ryan, but you have to remember, that was almost two thousand years ago. But I guess once we know how to hug like a daddy, it just never goes away! That was a pretty cool entry you made into Crown Hall. I've seen plenty of happy entries into this place, Ryan, but I reassure you, yours will be talked about forever! Let's get on down the hall here to join Jesus in conference room 201."

Ryan laughed hard and smacked a fiver on St. Andrew's palm.

"Hi guys." Jesus said as He gathered water glasses for the four of us.

Ryan and I greeted Jesus, then I laid the flowers on a coffee table at the back of the room.

"Ryan," asked St. Andrew, "would you like to have a look around the area while I speak to Jesus about a trip I'm making tomorrow?"

"I would love to," answered Ryan.

"Thank you, Ryan."

"Jesus," said St. Andrew, "St. Matthew has that trip to Brazil planned for tomorrow. The big festival down there begins the next day, so we want to be in place ahead of time, before sunset. Those missionaries have been praying, so lots of us are going to hit the area hard, fishing for new souls. Everyone is excited and we're launching from the south end of the balcony."

"And I've already been down and escorted several thousand angels to provide a holy presence to the city," I added.

"It couldn't be planned any better than that. "Thank you all so much."

We three turned and watched Ryan look around the conference room at the pastel scenes of heaven painted on the walls, very similar to those in the Great Hall. One painting was of a large circle of holy kids and Jesus holding hands, their heads lifted high in praise to God. In the middle of the circle were picnic baskets filled with food. Ryan noticed a dark ring on the ground around the picnic baskets. As he stepped closer, he saw that the dark ring was a circle of ants holding hands and praising God too! He laughed out loud and remembered that God was the Creator of everything.

Ryan walked to a nearby window and looked out. He could see two men fly-fishing in a distant stream, and he felt sure that heaven was the reward for all who trust that Jesus Christ is their personal Savior, trust that God is in control, and trust that everything written in the Holy Bible is true. Ryan had trusted all these things when he had lived on earth, and, because of it, he could forever fly, fly-fish, and fish for new souls.

Turning his attention back to the room, Ryan saw a huge, long cherrywood conference table surrounded by beautiful chairs in the center of the room, and a few other seating areas nearby.

"This conference room is not like the one at my dad's office. He had inboxes for paperwork and contracts, and there were phones and flat-screens and a sound system. My favorite things there were his ink pens and Post-it notes," observed Ryan. "My dad carried a backpack and a cell phone, but I don't see those things, either."

"Is heaven online, Jesus? Do you have a website? An Eddress? Do the saints surf the net?"

Jesus saw another perfect teaching moment, and answered, "This is heaven, the home of wisdom, knowledge, and communication, Ryan. Lawsuits, dishonesty, cheating, and paper cuts aren't found in heaven, because they are not of God. We don't sign contracts because this is the birthplace of trust and agreement, the place of perfect memory. We don't have a shredder, Post-it notes, flat-screens, or secrets. I wear a crown, not a backpack. And I hold charity, not a cell phone."

We could see the wheels turning in Ryan's head.

St. Andrew added, "And about the website, God is more powerful than the Internet, and Heaven is the original home page. God e-mails, texts, tweets, and messages using His Holy Spirit, and the Holy

Spirit communicates to the human heart, inviting the lost to salvation through Christ."

With this new perspective and what he had just seen at the balcony, Ryan smiled and said, "Okay, I get it. So the holies who 'surf' and 'message' from the balcony..."

"Have been doing it for centuries, Ryan, since God created man, and long before the Internet," Jesus added with a smile. So while we have this conference room, its primary use is to meet with new holies and finalize plans for mission trips to earth."

"I am thankful to be here, Jesus, and I am listening," responded Ryan.

8

THE QUEST

Beside a window in the back corner of the conference room, four wing-back chairs were arranged around a coffee table. A breeze entered the glassless window and blew Jesus' robe. After pouring the water into glasses on the table, He motioned to Ryan, St. Andrew and me, calling, "Come sit with Me."

Ryan bounced right over and curled himself into the chair closest to Jesus. He tucked one foot beneath his body and sank deep into the cushion. St. Andrew and I took the remaining chairs.

Jesus offered each of us a refreshing glass of water. Ryan took his into both hands and drank it down as he watched us from above the crystal rim. He finished with a loud final swallow and let out the deep breath he'd been holding. A couple of short pants followed, and he wiped away a water mustache with his tongue and then set the empty glass down.

"I really like that painting of the praising ants," Ryan said, pointing across the room. "I loved art class in school. My mom always stuck my pictures on our refrigerator. But one year for my birthday, she and my dad gave me back four of the very best ones in frames. Dad hung them all around the house because Mom said she felt happy when she looked at them."

"You will meet the artist who painted that picnic scene," Christ said. "On earth, he was famous for painting children. In his later years, he enjoyed teaching art classes at his studio and would tell people about My love for little children."

"And he has a studio here," St. Andrew added, "and teaches holy kids to paint. I have a son here who is eight years old, Ryan, and he paints there. He and Angela call themselves 'partners in paint.' So when you return from your mission I will introduce you to him."

"I'm already looking forward to that. Speaking of Angela, she told me something cool. May I tell you?"

"Sure. Remember we have no secrets here," Christ answered looking around at us, then back to Ryan.

"I know why she's so good at flying - she's been here for two hundred years!" Ryan said.

Jesus looked at me.

"It's true," I answered. "Her brothers, sisters, cousins, aunts, uncles, and grandparents, many generations of her family, are here. As God called each of them to heaven, I retrieved and delivered their set of wings to St. Peter at the landing. But, of course, I delivered them only for those family members who became born again."

"She just left to meet them at a praise gathering," Ryan proclaimed. "She's probably with them by now."

"Yes, there's always a praise gathering at the River Jordan," Jesus said. "You're going to love that praise rally, Ryan. The songs are sung with and without music and anyone can play an instrument or sing a solo. So you could play your violin there."

"If I had it," Ryan said, laughing.

St. Andrew laughed and told Ryan about a special shop where instruments were made.

"In fact," Jesus said, "My earthly father, Joseph, is a carpenter there. He can make a violin that's just the right size for you. You can ask Angela to take you there."

"I'm sure she knows where to find it," Ryan responded. "She really knows her way around. How old was she when she came to heaven?"

"Twelve, just like you," Christ answered.

"Oh," he replied, liking the idea of having that in common with her.

"Well, she's pretty cool for a girl," he confessed. "Before the feast, she took me for flying lessons, then to the Crystal Sea, and afterward we went to this incredible park. It had a sports complex, homes, animals, and holy people everywhere. Then, on our way here, she showed me the balcony." His lips pronounced the word 'balcony' with great animation.

Christ laughed and said, "She spends a lot of time at the balcony watching and encouraging kids. She used to watch you run and loved to listen to your prayers. She believed your strong sense of right and wrong was a good influence on your friends and family. When she learned you were coming, she could hardly wait to meet you and teach you to fly."

Ryan was all smiles as he said, "I can hardly wait to hang at the balcony with her and encourage friends and my brothers."

"Do you want to hear some exciting news about your brothers?" St. Andrew asked.

"Oh, yes," Ryan shouted!

"They say precious prayers at bedtime and in church, and they both invited Christ into their hearts."

"Yes!" His arms motioned a big pullback. He was so thrilled to hear this excellent news that he had to grip the sides of his chair to hold himself down.

"Thank You, Jesus! Glory to God," Ryan replied.

"You witnessed well to them, Big Brother Ryan." Jesus laughed. "Their love for God is very deep in ones so young."

"I wouldn't want them to miss heaven. And I wouldn't want to miss spending eternity with them."

"They shall be strong witnesses to their friends like you and Angela were," Christ added.

"How old was Angela when she became a Christian?" Ryan inquired.

"She was eight years old and quickly became a missionary." St. Andrew began. "She led most of her family to Christianity except for her parents. They chose not to believe what she shared about Christ. They became so embarrassed and angry about her witnessing everywhere that they eventually kicked her out of their home.

"For the next four years she lived on the streets of London and witnessed to everyone she saw, including other homeless people, but especially to orphans. And many of those children are here because Angela led them to Christ. She spread the good news that God loved them and cared about what happened to them. Her heart was big for children but completely broken for her parents' love and their salvation."

Christ added, "One of the reasons she spends so much time at the balcony is to encourage children and parents, whole families, to become born again so they can be together for eternity."

Ryan considered this for a moment and then said, "Angela spent four years without her parents?"

Christ nodded his head.

"I remember the summer when I was nine years old," Ryan began. "I went by myself to Colorado and spent a week with my cousins. We went swimming in the lakes, saw two pro ballgames, and went camping in the mountains. The daytime was great fun, Jesus, but every night I was sad and cried myself to sleep because I missed my family. I was really homesick for them."

Jesus smiled. "I remember that. You prayed every night, asking me to watch over them. And I did, Ryan. Then I made sure you got home safely to be reunited with them. They had missed you and prayed for you too. But all was well when you and your family were reunited."

"I was so glad to see my parents at the airport that I cried, and they cried too."

The room fell silent for a moment, as Ryan was thinking.

"So, Jesus…" Ryan untucked his foot and scooted to the very edge of his seat. "I know that only born-again believers get into heaven. But what about when kids die and come to heaven, but their parents never become born again? Will those families ever be completely reunited? Will those parents ever see their kids again?"

"What do you think, Ryan?" Christ had answered with a question.

Between thumb and finger, Ryan rolled a bit of his robe and thought. "Well, what about Angela's parents?" he asked.

"They did not arrive in heaven when they died on earth," Christ answered.

"She just told me that they would not be at the River Jordan praise gathering. Does she know where they are?"

"Yes, Ryan, we all do."

He stopped rubbing his robe and looked straight into the Savior's face. "Well, is she homesick for them? She must be sad. Does she cry for them?"

"No, Ryan," Christ answered. "Angela is not homesick for her earthly parents. In heaven, we are made whole, perfect, and complete. Angela cried for her earthly parents when they rejected Me, but after they died, nothing could be done for them. There is no sadness in God's heaven. Sadness is the feeling humans have when they experience loss or disappointment on earth. Heaven has no loss or disappointment, only blessing and gain. We *are* able to feel grief when, from the balcony or on missions, we see people in need of God but who choose to reject Him. God is the difference between real love and sadness, the difference between life and death. Just as life is the time when sadness can be felt, it is also the time to become born again."

"Sadness, like time," Christ continued, "was created for life on earth but does not exist in heaven. Time and sadness teach humans to want things to be loving and correct. When humans are aware of love and tired of mistakes, they strive to find a place where there is peace. They soon realize that no place on earth is without mistakes and sadness. That's when they look for a savior, someone who can strengthen them in their situation and give them peace. God deals with each person when he or she comes to this point in his or her life. That's when the person becomes God conscious, and the Holy Spirit urges them to go forward and seek God."

"There comes a time, Ryan, when each person must decide if he or she is for God or against Him. Those who choose Him become saved or born again into a new life of hope, of salvation and of better things to come. At the point of their salvation, I send the Holy Spirit to their heart and mind to lead and guide them. If they will begin to read the Bible and faithfully attend church to hear good truth, they can be encouraged and learn to trust that We are always there for them, helping them through hard times."

"But many reject the idea of serving God, their Creator. They are the very ones who do not spend eternity here, and that includes Angela's parents."

Ryan stood and ran, pointing out the window. "Who on earth…I mean how could anybody say no to Christ and salvation and eternal life if they knew what was here? Who would want to miss out on heaven?"

With a nodding head, Jesus placed His fingertips together and settled back in His chair. St. Andrew joined Ryan at the window and answered, "That's just it, Ryan. They don't know what is here. They will not listen long enough to know that trusting and following Lord Jesus Christ is the only way into heaven. They won't read the Bible enough to know that life in heaven is just the opposite of the difficulties that can be found on earth. They don't know how, or don't want to know how to have a personal relationship with Jesus. Everybody, Ryan, wants to live forever in a perfect place, but some are too self-centered to give Christ charge of their lives. Others are just too lazy to be obedient." He placed his arm around Ryan's shoulder and walked him back to his chair, where Ryan stood and listened.

"You see, Ryan," he said, "everybody wants a savior, but not everybody wants a lord."

Ryan again paused for a quiet moment, and then asked, "Jesus?"

"Yes, Ryan?"

"What is it like for those who die without You and can't come to heaven?"

"Remember being homesick for your family while you were in Colorado?" Christ asked.

"Yes." Ryan fell back into the wingback, remembering that miserable separation.

"If people reject Me and die unsaved, they will be eternally separated from God, from love, and from peace. They will be forever alone and will experience death and darkness for eternity."

Ryan looked toward the window and said, "Imagine being forever separated from heaven. Now that I've experienced it, I think of those on earth not bound for heaven, and I feel deeply for them. If they don't come here they will miss their purpose. They won't meet their guardian angels or learn to fly. They won't feast with the saints or see that golden key in St. Peter's pocket. They won't meet the Savior or be hugged by the arms of God. They won't laugh or celebrate in *their* eternity."

He turned to Jesus and said, "What can I do, Lord? What can I do to help? Whatever my mission is, if it helps even one lost person to know You, I'm ready to go."

Full of concern, Ryan fell to his knees before the Lord Jesus. "Here am I, Lord. Send me. Send me!"

Christ held Ryan's face in His gentle hands. Smiling, He responded, "You are ready indeed, Ryan Allen. You are full of God's Holy Spirit with grief and compassion stirring deep inside you. It is time to receive your instruction."

"With full empowerment of God's Holy Spirit, We are sending you to encourage the children in your hometown, Keyota. Many of them are surrounded by an evil, blinding darkness, which discourages and confuses them, and they do not see the light of God. I shall soon return to earth to claim My own, but only those who are born again in the spirit of God. I want those Keyota children to be included. The darkness of sin there must be brightened. Without the light of God's spirit, they can never find their way to heaven. But you will take the light, and speed your way to touch thousands of lives in a short amount of time. Remember, time is drawing close for My second coming, so let the quickened spirit encourage them to choose God."

"But how will I know where to find them?" Ryan inquired.

"Listen for the prayers of the youth," Christ said. "Spend time with those who pray, and you will discover your opportunities for encouragement. You can go anywhere to find or follow the youth. Especially be on the lookout for large youth gatherings. Know that your words of encouragement can make the difference as to where they spend eternity."

St. Andrew stepped over to Ryan, and with Christ they laid their holy hands upon Ryan's head, and I bowed my head. Together they spoke, "God's truth be known and trusted. God's kingdom be increased."

The saint and Savior stood and helped the holy kid to his feet.

"You will see many guardians watching over and helping people," St. Andrew instructed. "But remember, Ryan, with the strength of God's Holy Spirit, your words of truth are a mighty force to the hearts and minds of humans. Follow where the Holy Spirit takes you. God and I can always hear your thoughts and feel your emotions, and while you're on mission, so can every holy person at the balcony."

Gabriel added, "And God has assigned me a special task to be your constant watch-guard while you're on your first mission. From my tower, I will never take my eyes away from you, and I, too, will be able to hear your thoughts, and feel your emotions."

Knowing that this meeting was over, Ryan turned and led the way through the foyer and down the stairs to the open double doors. He bid us good-bye and lifted off the front porch of Crown Hall, heading for the balcony.

Watching him fly, we looked at one another and said in unison, "He's a balcony dweller."

I returned to my tower and focused on Ryan with great enthusiasm. This was going to be good!

9

REENTRY

There was no flight plan to be filed in heaven, no clearance for takeoff granted from workers in glass towers. There was no waiting his turn to taxi down a runway before taking to the real friendly skies. Ryan already had permission to take off; Jesus said so. There was air traffic in heaven, but the flying holies saw one another and made simple adjustments like scooting over a little before passing.

At last the balcony was in sight. Ryan saw holies and angels dropping down and through, on their way to work a mission no doubt. That quickening struck his wings again, and Ryan spread them wide. He did a fast flyover of the area and then dove headfirst down through the opening as fast as he could.

The air that rushed over his body was fresh. It was cool air without bugs to smack his face or fly down his throat like they sometimes did when he rode his bike. The balcony's mist felt good and added pleasure to his thrilling, weightless dive. He felt a wave of butterflies in his stomach, and his lungs filled with heaven's pure air. By the time he let out the air, he was no longer in the perfect heaven but was streaking down through space and entering earth's atmosphere.

As his body sank closer to the planet, he met the old, familiar smell of dirt and water. The stench was strong, and gravity pulled heavily on his body.

As he moved closer, Ryan could hear cries of sad despair from the ungodly, evil demons who roamed about, looking for their next soul to confuse, depress, or destroy.

"Keep going," Christ spoke to him from heaven. "Stay focused. To your left is North America, and you can find Kansas. Look for a nice place to rest while you wait for night to fall and then enter the city."

Ryan continued dropping closer to earth and banked left. He saw the sunlight glistening on the Atlantic Ocean and then rivers that sprawled across the land like crippled fingers.

Cities dotted the landscape. Then he could see a huge golden mass spread across the land like peanut butter on bread, only this golden mass swayed in unison with the wind. Ryan's grin stretched from ear to ear. He had found his way to Kansas, where the golden fields of wheat reflected earth's sunlight on his face.

He touched down beside a narrow river and decided to take his rest there. It would be easy to find Keyota once dusk arrived and darkness set in. The glow of the streetlights, aircraft-manufacturing plants, and the many landing strips would lead him to where his job awaited.

But for now, Ryan wet his feet in the river and skipped small, flat rocks across the water while he waited on the sandy shore.

10

SCOOT

A big, orange moon rose in the east and made its way higher into the evening sky over Kansas, dragging stars along with it. Ryan stood and stretched his body. He brushed off his robe and flicked his wings to free them of dried sand. Then he took flight, rising high above the wheat fields, eastbound in search of those bright city lights.

Keyota seemed to shine like a new penny on asphalt. No angel, nor even this new holy kid, could miss it. But as breathtaking as the lights were, as glad as he was to be in his old hometown, what really thrilled Ryan was the sound of praying voices.

Ryan slowed his speed as he entered the air space above the city. He listened to the cries and praises of the people and felt joy as he heard Christians thanking God for His help.

But these voices, nearly all of them, were the voices of the very young or very old. Few were those of the youth—very few, but there were some.

Ryan singled out one praying voice and followed it down through a roof and an attic to a basement bedroom. There he found a blond-headed teenage boy who was kneeling and talking to God. A black Labrador retriever sprawled across the bed, half asleep. Ryan counted seventeen guardian angels, on bended knees, praying along. Ryan perched himself on the footboard of the old brown bed, where his feet could swing. He petted the old dog and listened to the prayer.

"And, Lord, thank You for sending so many kids to Bible club today. I counted forty—just forty out of the two thousand kids at my school. Help us to reach out to the others at Keyota Plains High School who need You."

"Most of the kids at our school don't know You. I heard today that Hunter Kemp is really down and getting into some bad stuff. I've tried to talk to him, Lord, but You know how angry he is over his father's death. He won't speak to me or anybody else."

"I gave You my heart, Jesus, and I want to do Your work. Please send me someone to witness to soon. Will You put that person right in front of me and make it obvious that he or she is the one? Please, Lord, just give me one set of listening ears. In Jesus' name I pray. Amen."

Seventeen startlingly loud "amens" followed. Ryan had to laugh as he, the guardians, and the dog could hear the shout, but the boy could not.

As the boy stood and put away his Bible, the guardians scrambled to get out of his way. He picked up a sports bag and stuffed it with shorts, socks, and a shirt. He removed a shattered pair of shin guards from the bag and tossed them into the trashcan and then opened a new box. With a red marker, he began writing on the inside. Ryan jumped up to read what the boy wrote. It was the name Scoot.

"Scoot," Ryan shouted. "Your name is *Scoot*? Where did you get a name like that?"

"Yep. I'm glad my parents gave me a short nickname," Scoot mumbled aloud and glanced at the dog. "It's quick to write, and it's easy for people to remember."

The dog's thick tail lifted and then slammed against the comforter as if to acknowledge his boy's comment. Scoot stuffed the shin guards into the bag.

"OK," he continued mumbling. "Tomorrow is Wednesday, so practice ends at five. It's my day to collect dirty towels from the showers and take them down to the laundry room in the basement under the boys' gym. I better remind Mom to pick me up late."

Ryan watched as Scoot stuck his head out of the bedroom door and yelled up the stairs. "Mom! Dad! Can you come pray me goodnight?"

The holy kid flew out of that house with new excitement. And Ryan would go to Keyota Plains High School and hang out. He would pick out a hurting someone for Scoot, maybe that guy named Hunter Kemp. But for now, there were other people in Keyota to help.

Ryan spent the rest of that night, and some of the next day, listening to prayers, comforting, helping, and speaking words of hope to all who prayed. He comforted a girl soccer player who broke her ankle at practice, visited seven foster-care families, and broke a cigarette lighter that two kids used as a toy. Hearing church bells ringing, Ryan followed the sound and perched himself on top of a cross in the yard, and he prayed, thanking God for His abundant goodness.

11

THE TINY SPEEDO

In the afternoon, Ryan had just left a church Bible club where seven kids had prayed to receive Christ before going home. His volunteers, praying and praising God for sending the Holy Spirit so strongly, surrounded the Pastor. As the adults packed their cars to drive home, Ryan flew out, heading toward the sound of more praying youth.

But in the sky, he stopped short when he spotted a toddler running out of his back door and into the yard. A tiny red Speedo covered his bottom, the waistband resting snugly under a round belly.

As fast as his legs would carry him, he headed toward the open gate of the fence surrounding a large swimming pool. He laughed and pointed to his toys floating on the water and made excited baby talk.

His tiny feet sped toward the deep end, where he stopped and, like boys do, pumped his knees and then leapt toward the water.

All the other times he had jumped in, the little boy's father had been there to catch him. But today his daddy was not at home, and Ryan could hear his mommy on the phone asking about horoscopes and tarot cards.

As fast as the white wings could carry him, Ryan flew toward the child. Although two guardians were quickly on their way to catch him, Ryan was faster. The child's last pump had given him a tiny spring upward, and that's when Ryan's hands grabbed the skimpy red Speedo and hooked it tightly on the edge of the ladder.

Now by his side, the guardians thanked Ryan and praised God for blessing him with speed the likes of which they'd never seen.

A shrill screech of disappointment filled the air as the would-be swimmer kicked his legs and pounded the water with baby fists. He was going nowhere fast, and Ryan stayed there to make sure.

The baby's wailing cry brought the mother flying out of the house. Her phone sailed through the air as she shrieked, "Oh! Oh my God! Oh, no! My baby!"

By the time the mother reached the baby, she was crying hysterically. The baby continued wailing and held out his arms to her. Quickly she grabbed him, and they clung together.

"Oh, I thank my lucky stars that you're all right," she told him.

Ryan listened while the mother told her child how precious he was and that she was sorry for not watching him closely.

In a nearby chair, the two rested and renewed their bond. The mother realized that the caught swimsuit was not a coincidence. It could be nothing less than a miracle. Her heart began to soften, and silent tears streamed down her cheeks.

"There aren't any lucky stars, lady. In fact, there's not any *luck* at all." Ryan sat on top of a table beside them, legs crisscrossed, arms resting in his lap. "So don't call those psychic phone lines anymore. There is a listening God, who loves you and watches over you and your baby. He has a perfect plan for your life and wants the very best for you and your family. I'm really sure everything that happens to you in life is either sent directly to you by God or that He allows it to happen so you will turn to Him. There's either God's protection or there's evil. Today, God sent me here to protect your baby. He is trying to get your attention."

Just then a neighbor came running toward the pool. When the mother saw her coming, she called out, "Ann! Oh, Ann, while I was inside on the phone, Jon ran out here alone and jumped into the pool. He would have drowned if his swimsuit hadn't hung on this ladder." She sobbed and pointed to it. "I thanked my lucky stars a minute ago, but, Ann, something tells me it wasn't lucky stars that did it. Something tells me it was that God you're always trying to tell me about." She continued crying. "Tell me about Him, Ann. I'll listen to you now."

Ann's arms hugged the woman, and she said, "First, let's pray."

Ryan knew that God was at work there, and he was thankful. As he quickly took off, a tiny white feather blew off his wing, and it slowly drifted down and landed on the shoulder of Ann, who ministered to her lost friend.

12

GIRLFRIENDS

Two teenage girls sat on a porch swing holding hands. One of the girls was praying, and the other one was crying. Ryan flew straight to them and nestled himself on the back of their swing among the band of praying guardians. With the day growing dark with clouds, the wind was whipping from the southwest. Thunder and lightning fast approaching, Ryan listened to the prayer.

"Thank You, God, for sending Jesus to offer us eternal life. Thank You for saving me. Tonight, Roxie and I are asking you, Jesus, to give her faith to trust You as her Savior. She wants to invite You into her heart, but she's just not sure if You're real. Please give her faith, Lord. Help her to see that You love her. Please speak to her heart and let her know that You are the living God who has a plan for her life. In Christ's name we pray. Amen."

"What a powerful prayer," Ryan said to Roxie. "You should thank your friend for caring so much for you." He knew that his words would be her thoughts.

"Thanks, Megan. Your prayers are always so powerful. If I just had some kind of proof, you know, that Jesus was real. I don't know what it will take. I just wish I could trust like you do."

Lightning flashed, followed by a loud clap of thunder.

"Well, I'll never stop praying for you, Roxie."

"Thanks, but I have to go; it's beginning to sprinkle," she said and then hugged Megan.

Roxie walked to her bike and hopped on; she strapped on her helmet and backpack. Shaking her head, she called back to Megan, "Where on earth do you get all that faith? See you at school tomorrow."

Megan waved good-bye and prayed, asking God to somehow give Roxie faith. She could see Roxie's ginger hair blowing in the wind as the bicycle picked up speed. She could see the backpack sway from side to side as the pedals were pumped round and round. Through tears and raindrops, she could see another day ending and her best friend still without eternal life with God.

But what Megan couldn't see was Ryan mounted backward on the handlebars of the bike, practically in Roxie's face. She couldn't hear him tell Roxie how that night, in her dreams, she would see the kingdom of heaven and meet Jesus, that guy who loved her so much. And she didn't hear Ryan shout back to her that Roxie would ring her doorbell at six in the morning with tears of excitement, anxious to take those steps to salvation.

Surrounded by the fifteen guardians, Megan quietly returned to the porch swing. She wondered if Roxie would ever come and ring her doorbell, searching for Jesus.

13

THE ABORTUARY

A massive thunderstorm with lightning, hail, and high winds had been saturating New Mexico, Texas, and Oklahoma for a full day and was headed for Kansas. A local radio station had predicted that it would enter Keyota by three o'clock and bring torrential rain for the following twenty-four hours or longer. A southwest wind toyed with tree branches like a kid with a yo-yo, and the smell of rain was served to the city. Dogs in backyards paced, and the elderly swallowed aspirin for their achy joints.

Raindrops that came to Kansas were the size of Ping-Pong balls and could produce small streams with currents in the sewers and conduits of the city in ten minutes. These gully washers cleared the city pipes of dead rodents like skunks, rats, snakes, or other unpleasant varmints.

God has a way of making good come out of even the saddest event. And though the storm headed for Keyota would cause expensive damage to homes and property, it would also save one certain tiny life.

Three hours into the storm, Keyota had received six inches of rain. Hail had broken windows, dented cars, and redesigned the roofs of 432 houses. Local police had recorded seventy-four vehicle accidents, and hospital emergency rooms were filling up with the injured.

Trees were downed, and power outages blackened large sections of the city. The wind whipped through the streets at seventy-three miles per hour.

Old folks wrapped in shawls lit candles and reminisced about comparable storms and of Dust Bowl days. Millennials and Boomers moved their minivans and SUVs into their garages and ate leftovers. Babies cried or slept right through the thunder, while the downtown homeless checked into shelters.

Ryan leaned against the northeast wall of a large abortion clinic, chewing on a long piece of dried grass. The roof's wide overhang, combined with the southwest wind, created a dry spot for him to stand. He had a perfect view of a large concrete ditch lined with hedges and filled with swiftly moving rainwater.

Wedged between two hedges was a rain-soaked cardboard box that was home to a white female cat just beginning her labor pains. Ryan watched as she panted, grunted, pushed, and then rested. The frequent lightning and vibrating thunder added no comfort to her misery.

Yesterday, dry and secluded, the cardboard box was the best place she could find to give birth to her tiny kittens. But the glue that once held the box together was now dissolving. The box top had bent in half, and the sides were giving way, about to collapse. This laboring mama cat would have to move on and find a new home for the kittens soon to be born.

Confused and hurting, she didn't know of a better place to go. But Ryan did. Another act in God's perfect plan was about to take place. The time had come to make his move.

His eyes glued to the rain-soaked box, Ryan threw down the Johnson grass and spit like a ballplayer about to hit a homerun. At the box, he bent down, gently lifted the mama cat to her feet, and said, "There's a dry spot under the front steps of this building. It's higher ground there, and it's the most perfect place for you to give birth to your babies. It's where God wants you."

Of course, the cat couldn't understand Ryan's words, but just as he spoke them, she had the great idea of moving herself to a dry spot under the front steps of the building.

The next day, the sun was out, and the city had begun to restore itself from storm damage and flooding. Power had been restored to parts of the city, and it was business as usual for most, including the local abortuary. It opened its doors just as BeccAnne, a sixteen-year-old high-school sophomore, opened her vanity drawer at home and carefully chose a pink lipstick for the day. She was thirteen weeks pregnant and had a four o'clock appointment.

Her eighteen-year-old boyfriend had begged her to have an abortion. He felt that a child in his life right then would interfere with his college plans. He confided in his father, who told BeccAnne that there was nothing to an abortion; it was just tissue being removed. Then he supplied the money and booked the appointment to have his grandchild aborted.

Things happened so fast that BeccAnne didn't have much time to think about what she wanted. But in her heart, she knew what grew inside her. It was a baby. She knew that if she did not have the tissue removed as scheduled, in six months she would give birth. Each morning as she rose and each night as she slipped into her footed pajamas, she wondered how it could be just tissue if a child came out of it. Now more than ever, BeccAnne needed her mother, but this news would certainly break her heart.

The day of her appointment had come, and she drove to the abortuary all by herself—but not alone.

Jam-packed in the front and back seats, and attached to the door handles, and bumpers of her car, were holy kids and a few iridescent-winged baby angels. They were there to encourage BeccAnne to let her baby live.

BeccAnne considered turning her car around and heading back home, but how would she ever explain that decision to her boyfriend and his dad? She kept on driving. Knowing that she was about to take part in an unspeakable event, she felt her heart grow heavy, and felt its beat all over her body.

Arriving at the clinic, she parked her car and recounted the cash in her purse. Yes, it would be enough to eliminate one small life to keep another life simpler. As she replaced the money, her hands shook, and her teeth chattered.

Tears of sadness welled in her eyes as she entered the private gate and unconfidently made her way through the shady courtyard toward the front porch of the clinic. There, holy moms and dads surrounded her and walked with her. They urged her to leave this place of evil and let the little one be born.

BeccAnne stopped at a wooden bench near the front porch, deciding to rest a moment and collect the thoughts that seemed to bombard her. Her mind was swirling with thoughts. Confused, she pulled tissues from her pocket and sobbed.

Ryan sat down beside her, his holy hand patting her back, and he spoke. "There's a precious baby growing inside you who needs to be born. God has a special plan for your future, BeccAnne, and he has chosen a loving, Christian man and wife to adopt your child. This baby needs to be born to fulfill the plan God has for him. Great blessings are in store for you, too, but you must go now from this place of destruction and pray."

When BeccAnne came up for air, she wiped away tears and whispered to her unborn child, "You are a special gift from God, little one."

For the first time, she felt her child move within her. Then she knew without a doubt that there was a child, alive, growing and waiting to be born.

"And look at me," she said. "I was about to throw you away. I am so sorry," she cried.

Through her tears, she confessed, "God, I can't do this on my own. If You're really there, I'll need Your help more now than ever. Will You help me tell my parents? Will You help me find that Christian man and wife that You have chosen to raise this child?"

Just then she saw a white cat enter the courtyard and head straight for her. The cat rubbed against BeccAnne and let out a loud meow before it slipped under the open porch. BeccAnne loved cats. She smiled and watched as it nestled in among a litter of seven tiny kittens that immediately began nursing.

BeccAnne's spirit was restored to joy. She knew the cat's meow had to be a message from God. If He would take care of those tiny kittens in last night's storm, she knew that He would always be there for her.

Standing, she gathered her purseful of money and walked back to her car. As she opened the car door, holies scattered to clear a spot for her. Ryan stood outside and helped her shut the door. He leaned inside the car window and said, "Pray for God's wisdom, BeccAnne. Read His Word and pray every day. And never forget to listen for the still, small voice."

As she drove toward home, BeccAnne felt that her heart was no longer heavy. She felt God's Holy Spirit right beside her.

14

TEAM DESTINY

Ryan followed a voice that was mixed with prayer and crying. He flew down to the third floor of a hospital, where a teenager sat halfway up in his hospital bed. Alone in the room, he slowly wiped his tears away with the bed sheet. Across his chest lay an open Bible.

Ryan counted eighteen praying guardians on their knees about the room, so Ryan knew this boy was seventeen years old. The name 'Nicholas' was written on the whiteboard on the wall.

Ryan saw that a bag of orange liquid hung on a pole beside the bed. A tube ran from it and connected to the boy's chest. He noticed that Nicholas had no hair. There were dark circles under his eyes, and his cheekbones stuck out. His skin looked pale and gray, and his breathing was shallow. Ryan knew that Nicholas was really sick. He remembered that his great-uncle Chester had had cancer and lost his hair after receiving chemotherapy. He wondered if Nicholas had cancer too.

Ryan admired the roomful of balloons and cookie bouquets. There were green plants, and flowers packed on every shelf, plus get-well cards and posters with handwritten notes of love that covered the walls. On the nightstand beside the bed there was a small stack of colored brochures. Ryan read the bold print, "Students, do you know Christ? Attend 'Youth Truth' and meet Him." Below those words was a picture of a football stadium filled with teenagers. Ryan wanted to read more of the brochure, but Nicholas began praying again, so he quickly crawled onto the bed beside the boy, snuggled up close, and listened.

"Father, my baseball team, Destiny, has stopped coming to see me here. Dying is a scary thing for us humans, and they know that I am not going to live. I've told them my cancer has spread and that it won't be much longer."

"I know it's really hard for them to face me, to face one of their friends dying, and I can understand that. But they don't believe me when I tell them I'm not afraid to die. That's okay, Father, but what's not okay is that they don't believe in You."

"It breaks my heart, Lord God, that they don't know You. Soon I'll be healed in heaven with You, but they'll still be lost in this world. Who are You going to send to tell them about Jesus? They've got to meet Jesus! They gotta meet me up there someday, God. I just know heaven has a baseball diamond, and we have games yet to play. You know I'm ready to go with You, but what about my friends? Who's going to tell them about the way to heaven?"

At that moment, the hall outside Nicholas' room was filled with rowdy voices and squeaking tennis shoes on the floor. Several heavy knocks on the door pushed it wide open. Heads wearing baseball caps popped in, and many excited, uncontrolled voices filled the air.

The guardians shot quickly to the ceiling to make way for the dozen or more teenage boys who filled the room. Ryan saw several with raised hands getting ready to high five Nicholas. He knew that Nicholas could barely lift his hand to wipe tears, much less have the power to give and receive a healthy high five from these strong boys.

"Give 'em five," Ryan shouted, and then he assisted Nicholas's weak arm to meet the friendly blows that followed.

"Hey, man, what's up?" one asked.

"What's happenin', Nick?" another asked. Staring at the orange bag of liquid on the pole, he knew what was up, but he really didn't want to know what was happenin'.

Nicholas couldn't believe the strength brought on by just a visit from his buddies. He couldn't believe the power in his high five.

"You guys should come every day. You build me up." Nicholas smiled.

The feisty young men pushed and crowded into the room and made themselves at home. Three piled into the recliner, two in the straight-back chair. The rest stacked onto Nicholas' bed, barely missing Ryan, who quickly hovered up and over to the top of the bed for a full view of the room. His smiled and began to listen.

For the next hour and forty-five minutes, the guys in baseball caps reported, play-by-play, inning-by-inning, the details of how they had qualified that afternoon for baseball nationals in Tampa, Florida. Nicholas absorbed every last detail of their stories. He commented on every victory and laughed until he was exhausted. The team captain could see that Nicholas was really tired. Signaling the team that it was time to go, he tapped his watch and nodded toward the door, and then he told Nicholas that they needed to leave.

Through all the years that the Destiny team had played together, Nicholas had always insisted they pray before each game. He was known as Destiny's "pray boy." Tonight, again, he would live up to his name.

"Huddle up, men. Pray Boy's going to say it," said the captain.

The guys stood gathered around his bed and stacked their hands together. Ryan slid down the bed sheet beside Nicholas and added his hand to the heap. Then Nicholas prayed.

"Father, I thank You for every game we've played together. Thank You that we haven't lost a game in three and a half years. Thank You for healing our minor injuries, and thank You for all the safe travels."

"Tonight, God, this pray boy has just two last things to ask of You. First, for our team: please watch over these guys at the nationals; bless them individually and give them endurance for all the games; let them win; give them safe travel; bless the healthy food they eat; and please, Lord, let Florida be ready for them!"

Yells and hoots exploded in the room!

"And secondly, Father, please send Your Holy Spirit to lead them to know Christ as their personal Savior. We're a team here on earth, Lord, and someday we want to be a team in heaven."

There was a brief silence, and then Nicholas said, "In the name of Christ we pray. Amen."

No one wanted to be the first to pull his hand out of the stack; everyone knew this was the last time Nicholas would pray for them. Most of these guys were not believers in Christ, but they *were* believers in Nicholas' lucky prayers.

Always after Nicholas' prayer, the guys on the Destiny team would shout out "another win" then run onto the field. But tonight nobody shouted it; in fact, nobody moved a muscle. The hands remained in the center pile until one was forced to slide out to wipe away a humbled tear that had managed to escape.

Ryan was moved by their sadness, but remembering the brochures about "Youth Truth" that lay on the nightstand, he told Nicholas to hand them out to the guys.

"Oh, by the way, guys, before you leave, I have one last request to ask of you."

"Anything you ask, man." The captain's answer was followed by fourteen positive grunts.

"Over here on the table are some brochures my youth pastor brought me yesterday." Ryan helped Nicholas point to the brochures, and one of the guys handed the stack to him.

"There's going to be a one-evening youth retreat tomorrow night at the university," Nicholas continued, "and my last request of each one of you is that you will go."

Each team member took a brochure and promised Nicholas he would go.

"I'll go but just for you, Nicholas," one guy said.

Nicholas smiled and replied, "That's a good enough reason."

The team laughed, replaced their caps, and left the room a bit more quietly than they had entered. A few uttered the word "later," but not one could bear to say "good-bye."

"You're going to love heaven, Nicholas," Ryan said. "And you're right; there *is* a baseball diamond." He pulled the covers up high on Nicholas, gave him a hug, and flew out of the room the same way he entered.

15

THE SWIMMER

Ryan sat on the floor of a shadowy bedroom and leaned back against the dresser. Quietly, he admired the roomful of family photographs and swim trophies. Hanging on the bedpost was a dusty baseball cap with the Keyota high school logo and a swimmer icon on the front. Outside, a morning shower was ending.

Across from him, Hunter Kemp sat on the edge of his bed, almost alone in his room. The door was shut, lights off. His forehead rested in the palms of his hands, and his long, dyed black hair hung down between his fingers. Although his head was pounding from another drinking binge the night before, the clock radio by his bed blared out tunes from a local golden oldies station.

Hunter could identify with every negative song that station played, but the one playing now seemed to be his life's new theme song. It was the Stones "I Can't Get No Satisfaction." He could relate to its title.

Hunter was a six-foot-tall senior at Keyota Plains High School. His body had been sleek and trim when his team won the title of varsity swim champions the year before. His father, Jack Hunter Kemp, a world swim champion in the 1970's, had been his personal coach, role model, encourager, and best friend. They were always together, and friends teased that they must be attached at the hip.

Mr. Kemp assisted the varsity coach during practice and swim meets, and everyone was proud to have him there. He ordered custom caps for the team that had the school logo and a swimmer icon on the front.

It was true; nothing had ever separated Hunter from his father—nothing, that is, until a fifty-year-old drunk driver ran a red light, broadsiding Mr. Kemp's Jeep and killing him instantly.

Hunter never got to say good-bye. He never got to say thanks for everything, and he never got a minute to beg his father not to die.

But he did get to feel alone, abandoned, and angry. Then bitterness began to set in.

Hunter's soul dove to a new low and soaked in self-pity. In the deep pit of depression that Hunter had dug for himself, almost no one had been able to reach him. He had lost sixteen pounds of muscle mass, but who cared? His mother had arranged grief counseling for him, but after only three sessions, Hunter told her that therapy couldn't bring his dad back, and he refused to go again.

The high-school swim coach had made repeated attempts to meet with Hunter but to no avail. Hunter broke up with his sweet girlfriend, began cutting classes, and started smoking tobacco. Bottled spring water used to quench his thirst; now he preferred alcohol.

The only color in his wardrobe was black. His nails were bitten down to the quick, and his newly dyed hair was so black that it shined purple.

Hunter's winning attitude had always been a major positive influence on the team's spirit. He had clearly been their leader, but he quit the swim team and dumped his teammates. Mourning the death of Mr. Kemp had been difficult enough for those young men, but with the loss of Hunter from the team, they were now scattered and had become discouraged.

Lots of people had tried to help Hunter, but their words of encouragement fell on deaf ears. Only one guy, a lowly sophomore known as Scoot, had been able to get through to Hunter's soul.

This fast but cheesy little junior-varsity soccer player, who just happened to be a school Bible club leader, had caught Hunter crying in the basement of the boys' gym Wednesday after school.

Things hadn't gone well for Hunter that week. On Monday he had overslept and was running late, causing him to miss a little meeting with his drinking buddies before school. Then to make matters worse, his car hadn't started, so his mother made him ride the bus, where he got into a fight with a punk freshman who teased him. He skipped classes on Monday after lunch and got caught. His school counselor, Mr. Paul, a born-again believer, gave Hunter a detention for fighting and skipping, to be served Tuesday and Wednesday after school. He had to write a three-thousand-word essay on the theme "Why My Life is Great."

By Wednesday at five o'clock, Hunter was so angry that he bolted from the detention room and accidentally knocked down the principal in the hallway. She let him have it in front of everyone. At that point, he was so humiliated that he immediately had to find a remote place and let off steam.

Having spent the afternoon by Hunter's side, Ryan suggested the basement under the boys' gym, a suitable location for stress management. The basement door was nearby, so Hunter dashed in there and let loose with the waterworks. He had never cried at school before and, in general, hated basements. Why he chose to cry under the basement of the boys' gym, he would never know. Something just told him it would be the perfect secret place. Then Scoot, the soccer player, walked in with an armload of dirty towels. He saw Hunter standing alone with a face full of tears. Scoot must have known this might be his only chance to witness to Hunter, so he dropped the towels and took a deep breath.

At first Hunter had felt trapped and was forced to listen to Scoot. But then something told him to be still and listen. As the conversation went on, Hunter heard words like "deliverance," "peace," "salvation," and "healing."

Scoot told Hunter that he still had a father, a heavenly Father who loved him very much and had a perfect plan for his life. Scoot said that he couldn't make the pain go away, but he could show him where to find hope. Then he made Hunter, all six feet of him, bow his head while he prayed for peace and healing right there in the basement under the boys' gym in front of stacks of wet towels and rows of black-and-gold football uniforms.

Leaving Hunter where he'd found him, Scoot climbed the stairs leading from the basement. He never looked back, but he did call out, "Bible club meets Tuesday at noon in room M-1. Be there. Bring your lunch. I'm going to call you this weekend." Then the heavy door slammed shut.

Now here it was, Saturday morning, and this little incident was rocking Hunter's world. As he sat still on the edge of his bed, holding that throbbing head, his mother's cat, Cannonball, crawled from under the bed and rubbed against his leg. Hunter reached down to pet her, but Ryan was there and goosed the cat to make her jump up onto the nightstand. Her back paw hit the radio dial and instantly changed the station from the classic rock to a contemporary Christian radio station. The words of the song playing said, "I will not forget you."

The phone rang, but Hunter just sat and listened to the words of that song while hot tears rolled down his cheeks. The answering machine recorded a message. It was that praying, soccer-playing sophomore guy, Scoot. He said he'd be by that night at six thirty to pick Hunter up for Youth Truth, a one-evening Christian youth retreat at the local university football field. "Wear jeans and a jacket, but don't bother with an umbrella. Weatherman says it's clearing off."

Ryan told Hunter to pay close attention to that message. He said that Scoot was on the right track in life, that he loved God and would be a great friend who really cared.

Hunter replayed the message and listened again. What was it about this Scoot guy? He seemed more real than the others who'd tried to help. He talked about hope. There was definitely a spark about him, something trustworthy, familiar, and intriguing. Or maybe he'd just caught Hunt in a weak moment. Whatever. Hunter pulled his long sleeves over his hands and wiped his face dry. He flopped over on his pillow, eyes closed, and decided he would be ready at six thirty.

As he spread his wings for flight, Ryan thanked God for helping Hunter. Then he knocked the baseball cap off the bedpost and onto Hunter's face as he flew out of the house.

16

THE ANOINTING

The bright lights that illuminated an old university football stadium caught Ryan's eye. He buzzed by and hovered a moment, observing a large gathering, consisting of mostly young people, sitting in the stands. Ryan recalled Jesus's instruction to minister where there were large groups of teens. His wings tingled at the thought of this opportunity!

Hundreds of adults held hands and encircled the entire stadium property, assisted by a strong hedge of angels, who encouraged their trust in the Almighty. Ryan flew in closer and heard Christian praise music and singing voices. There were groups of young people and adults huddled together in the chill of the October evening, praying and inviting Jesus into their hearts. Then he realized that this must be Youth Truth.

From the stage, a minister invited any person who wanted to become born again to walk down from the stands and onto the field. Scores of Christian counselors were available to answer any questions they might have about becoming born again through Christ.

Ryan buzzed slowly over the crowd of thousands. As he looked closely, he saw Megan and her friend Roxie. Next he found the guys on Nicholas's baseball team, all fifteen of them.

"They came! They kept their promise to Nicholas," he shouted.

He saw BeccAnne and what must have been her parents; then he saw Scoot and Hunter and a large crowd of kids wearing black-and-gold jackets or baseball caps with a swimmer icon. Ryan remembered seeing the black-and-gold-colored uniforms in the basement of Keyota Plains High and knew that this group had to be their Bible club and maybe Scoot's soccer team. And those wearing the caps had to be Hunter's swim team.

"Thank You, God, for the power and influence of Your Holy Spirit," Ryan shouted toward heaven.

With hands lifted together in praise, the Christian leaders on the stage called out for a prompting of God's Holy Spirit on everyone present. They invited those who wanted to believe in Christ and become born-again believers to walk out onto the field and raise their hands.

Through the evening's message, including music and prayer, the seed of salvation had been planted. Now they asked God's spirit to cultivate it. Each teen would have to look within and decide whether he or she would stand for or reject the invitation to know God personally.

Ryan was empowered again. With all his might, he soared straight up toward heaven at a rate of speed known only to him and the Almighty. The tips of his wings burned to a refined shade of blue, and streaked across the clear night sky. Ryan was about to take Angela up on her offer to accompany him on this mission.

"Angela, come now and bring balcony dwellers with you," he shouted.

Angela and many balcony dwellers who had been watching the youth event that evening jumped over the balcony and blazed toward the stadium.

The youths who had stood jam-packed in the stands only moments before looked like they had turned to liquid as they poured out onto the field. Every square foot of the field, from goal post to goal post, quickly filled up with young people who wanted to meet the Savior and become born again. The night air was filled with raised hands, and the whole turf was covered. Not one blade of grass was visible from where God watched.

While the holies infiltrated the sky, the local barometric pressure rose sharply as the leaders called out for an anointing of the Holy Spirit. Although no clouds were in sight, the crowd of thousands saw a bolt of blue lightning streak across the sky, followed by a fine mist that fell on every head present. The anointing of the Holy Spirit had just taken place, and thousands of youths surrendered their lives and accepted Christ as their Savior.

Each teenager there, in one way or another, had spent his or her life searching for truth, honesty, and a reason to live. That night they met Jesus. That night they found hope. That night they were given someone to live for. That night they received a new life—of all places, in an old football stadium at a secular university.

Prayers to God had been answered, and praise to God was given. Ryan and the balcony dwellers were called back to heaven to join in the celebration. Thousands of tears of joy were shed as heaven rejoiced and praised the Almighty. There was dancing and cheering at the balcony. A celebration feast was held in the Great Hall. And at the landing of heaven, St. Peter opened the Book of Life and made a long entry of names. Through the blood of Christ, heaven's population continued to grow.

17

THE REWARD

At the celebration feast after Ryan's return, Christ had invited him to attend a ceremony at God's throne in the outdoor theater. Angela accompanied Ryan to the location, and the two entered all alone. There was a glow inside the amphitheater so bright that it was completely white. Ryan was nearly blinded as he tried to look around. The brightness was more intense than any light he had ever seen.

"This must be where halogen comes from," he said to Angela as his eyes began to adjust. Before him, he saw God's throne and the small, clear stream of water that flowed from it.

"Hello and welcome, My children," God spoke.

The two holy kids walked closer toward the throne, where they saw Jesus standing to the right and me, Gabriel, to the left. On a small table in front of them, Ryan saw a piece of gold from which the white light emanated.

God smiled and motioned for Ryan and Angela to come closer. Ryan examined the smile of the Almighty and said to Angela, "How can a smile say so much? How can just a smile tell me I am loved?"

"I have learned that love is the language of God, Ryan," she answered.

Naturally, in obedience to God, the two holy kids walked to His throne and bowed in reverence. Letting go of Angela's hand, Ryan stepped closer to inspect and saw the most beautiful crown he'd ever imagined. It was made of the same pure gold as St. Peter's key to the pearly gates and was covered in glistening colored stones and white pearls just like heaven's gate.

"Way cooler than Burger King's," he said to himself. He stood within inches of the crown, and he so wanted just to touch it.

"Go ahead," Jesus said.

Ryan's eyes shot to Jesus, and he shouted, "It's okay?"

"It's yours, Ryan. By fulfilling the plan God made for you, you have earned it."

Then God spoke. "All rise for this blessed occasion."

Ryan wondered who the "all" was, so he looked around. He saw all of heaven watching, waiting to witness yet another part of the Body of Christ fitting into place in heaven, receiving his just reward. His holy kid friends, thousands and thousands of them, were all down in front waving at him. He waved back. Then Ryan began to recognize other faces of people he'd known on earth.

First he saw Aunt Martha May and Uncle Chester, then Cousin Virginia, who came there when she was two years old. Next he recognized an old friend from kindergarten and his third-grade Sunday-schoolteacher, who encouraged him to invite Jesus into his heart. There was the cookie-baking neighbor, Mrs. McAlta, smiling and waving. He could almost taste the chocolate chips!

Then he noticed that they were all wearing golden crowns, and each was uniquely different from all the others. Some crowns were narrow golden bands that made him think they were wearing halos. Other crowns were wider and trimmed with small, brilliantly colored stones. And still others were wide, standing high on heads; some were so covered with diamonds that Ryan could barely see the gold that held them together.

"Angela! Everyone is wearing a crown," Ryan exclaimed. You're wearing one! I never saw the crowns before!"

That soft hand of Angela's slipped into his hand and pulled him down a couple of inches to the floor, then let go. He turned and looked at her.

"Receiving the crown is part of your reward," she began. "Every one of us goes on mission when we're new to heaven, and we each receive our crown when we return. But we are unable to see crowns until we have one of our own. That's a gift blessing from God."

"We've all stood where you are now, Ryan. After we finished our first mission to glorify God on earth, we stood in this very spot, and He rewarded us."

The Savior picked up the crown and handed it to Ryan. Ryan gasped and stared at it. He thought it would be heavy, but it was light. He checked it for loose stones, but they were all tightly fitted. On the inside was engraved the name "Ryan Allen." He wondered about the fit, so he quickly tried it on and found it was just the right size, like the wings and the robe that were made just for him. Ryan slipped it off and grinned.

"Cool! It fits, and God gave me my favorite colors."

Everyone laughed.

Jesus took the crown from Ryan and led him to God. Taking the crown from Jesus, God looked Ryan in the face and said, "You lived your life on earth with discipline. You practiced running with speed like your earthly father. You were obedient and followed the instructions of both of your parents. You were helpful to your brothers. When you sinned, you knew it and humbly asked to be forgiven. When you asked Me to guide you in doing what was right, you followed My instruction."

"'Run,' I told you. 'Run with all your strength.' Through your obedience in learning to run fast on earth, you became just the person I had planned for you to be. I took you from earth exactly when planned. Here, we instructed you in your purpose and sent you back to your hometown to minister to the many lost youth. You were quick, getting to a place of danger in time to catch the child's hand before he was injured. With My spirit, you worked to save the life of a special little one who otherwise would not have been born. And you encouraged thousands of the youth in Keyota to seek My Spirit and become born again. This crown of many jewels is your reward for obedience to Me."

God placed the crown on Ryan's head. "This is for a job well done. Thank you, My fine and faithful servant, Ryan Allen."

Ryan thanked his heavenly Father for life itself, for saving his soul, and for never abandoning him. He thanked God for hearing and answering prayers from people on earth who need Him, for His comfort and perfect love, for wisdom, and for all things in creation.

Ryan stood tall on his feet and reached up to feel the golden crown that, like his wings, instantly became a part of his body. Remembering a song he'd learned in Bible school, Ryan sang solo and a cappella, in praise to God Almighty.

As we all began singing praises, God looked at me, Gabriel, and whispered the name "Nicholas," so I took off to get his set of white wings, and St. Peter took off for the gate.

HOW CAN I BECOME A BORN-AGAIN CHRISTIAN?

First: I must accept that I am a sinner. "For all have sinned, and come short of the glory of God" (Romans 3:23).

Second: I must know that as a sinner, I owe a penalty. "For the wages of sin is death" (Romans 6:23).

Third: I must believe that Jesus Christ has already *paid* the debt for my sin debt "For when we were yet without strength, in due time, Christ died for the ungodly" (Romans 5:6).

Fourth: I must *receive* by faith what Jesus Christ has done for me. "But as many as received Him, to them He gave power to become the sons of God" (John 1:12).

I receive Jesus Christ by prayer:

Dear Lord Jesus, I know I am a sinner. I believe that Jesus died on the cross for me. I am willing to turn away from my sins and receive Jesus as my Savior and Lord. In Jesus's Name. Amen.

If you read these scriptures and prayed this prayer, sign your name and date anywhere on this page, and go tell your pastor or another believer.

ABOUT THE AUTHOR

Photo credit:

jennymyersphoto.com

Gwendolyn Siegrist holds a bachelor's degree in organizational leadership from Southern Nazarene University in Tulsa, Oklahoma. She currently holds a Kansas substitute teaching certificate.

Gwendolyn and her husband Larry have been married since 1978. Together, they have two adult children and are "Papa" and "Shushu" to five active grandchildren.

Gwendolyn wrote this book after losing many loved ones in a short period of time. She felt overwhelmed by grief, and she believes God gave her this story to help her heal and to encourage others devastated by loss. The purpose of this book is to help the bereaved focus on the wonderful truth that their loved ones are now in Heaven.

NOTES